THE SECRET

"Caitlin?" Rebecca's voice was faint. "Are you asleep?" she whispered, touching my arm.

I closed my eyes and tried to swallow the lump in my throat. I was too restless to fake sleep. "No. Not yet," I mumbled, rolling over and burying my head in the pillow.

Beside me, Rebecca sat up and clasped her knees to her chest. "Caitlin, I have never been so frightened in my life."

Me too! I wanted to tell her. But not of wolves. I was afraid of facing Nate in the morning . . . afraid the love might show on my face.

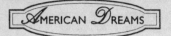

AMERICAN DREAMS

PLAINSONG
FOR
CAITLIN

ELIZABETH M. REES

AN AVON FLARE BOOK

PLAINSONG FOR CAITLIN is an original publication of Avon Books. This work has never before appeared in book form.

AVON BOOKS
A division of
The Hearst Corporation
1350 Avenue of the Americas
New York, New York 10019

For Richard, the heart of my heartland

Acknowledgments

I would like to extend my deepest thanks to some of the many people who helped me through the research on this book, making it possible:

To Ed Gilchrest at the New Bedford Whaling Museum in New Bedford, Massachusetts; Douglas Stein, Curator of Manuscripts at the Mystic Seaport Museum Library in Mystic, Connecticut; and in general I would like to thank other members of the staffs of both museums for helping me along the way.

For the Nebraska research, two people were immensely helpful: Mr. Jim Potter, the historian at the Nebraska State Historical Society, who told me about the blizzard of 1873; and Professor James Stubbendieck, a range ecologist at the University of Nebraska, who was amazed at a New Yorker's interest in wildflowers and prairies in general. He kindly provided me with the description of a prairie grass fire that helped kindle this book to life.

∽∽∽
Chapter 1

As long as I could remember, Mama's picture held the place of honor on our parlor mantelpiece. The miniature portrait, made by an itinerant painter who came to New Bedford one year, is surrounded by a lacy scrimshaw frame that Pa carved himself. When I was a little girl, I slipped into the parlor almost every day just to look at it. I wanted to know who my mother was and where I came from. But the picture only answered my questions with a smile. Sometimes there seemed such kindness in my mother's face, it made me ache.

One day the picture would belong to my older sister, Rebecca. Our father told us it would be our mother's wedding gift to her. Mama's miniature is almost the perfect image of Rebecca. They have the same high forehead, blond hair, and pale cheeks. Only the eyes, huge and smoky gray, are mine.

As our housekeeper, Molly MacGregor, always said, I am through and through a Jessup and my father's daughter. Molly, who has lived with us since I was a baby, was telling me so that cold November morning in 1871 when news of the great disaster first came in.

I was elbow deep in suds at the washtub. Though at sixteen I was old enough to be called a woman, I was still just a girl who longed more than anything to be a boy.

"Caitlin Jessup, you are the most headstrong mule of a girl I have ever met," Molly complained from over by the kitchen sink. "For sure you are your father's daughter."

"I wish I were my father's son!" I snapped back. Sweat trickled down my neck, and beneath my chemise my skin was drenched. My linsey-woolsey dress, which was so old I only wore it for washday, made me itch. "If I were a boy, I wouldn't be trapped inside this terrible hot kitchen, washing petticoats. I'd be off to sea with my pa!"

The autumn before, my father had signed up on a whaler bound for the Arctic—his first voyage in over twenty years. With the Atlantic whale schools almost fished out, ships like my father's journeyed clear around the tip of South America to reach the still bountiful whaling grounds of the Arctic. He planned to come back via San Francisco on the railroad. Still, he'd be gone at least two years. When he set sail Rebecca's fiancé, Ethan Nye, went with him.

"More likely, lass, men like your pa and Ethan would gladly trade places with you to get out of the bitter wind." Molly rinsed one of my petticoats in a wooden tub near the sink. "Mind you, a woman's work is just as hard and brave as any man's."

I doubted it. For the best part of my life, I'd been hearing how lucky I was to have been born a girl and not a boy. Boys younger than me set off to sea, slaving at the lowliest jobs aboard ship—and sometimes for a mean master at that. Though these days, most boys my age had given up on the sea entirely, going west instead to homestead or to prospect for gold. Sailing or homesteading, it all seemed better to me than a life where Monday was washday and Tuesday meant ironing, with Wednesday saved for sewing.

Molly held my second-best petticoat out at arm's length. In spite of my scrubbing, a broad band of gray soot still rimmed the hem. "What in the name of heaven have you done to this? Soon it'll be fit only for the ragbag."

I grabbed the petticoat from Molly and started scrubbing it again with a vengeance. "Boys' clothes are sturdier. If you'd only let me wear them, I'd—"

"A girl your age in boy's clothes! You'd be the laughingstock of New Bedford, Massachusetts." With great vigor Molly began putting a sheet through the wringer attached to the washbucket. "I will not let you disgrace the Jessup name just because your father was hardheaded enough to leave you and your sister to go on that wretched voyage. A fool's notion—that's what it is to think a man can still make a fortune whaling."

"What else could he do?" I leaped to my father's defense out of loyalty, but I had heard enough talk to know Molly was partly right. Whaling and whale oil had made New Bedford the richest city in the whole United States until, back in 1859, someone in Pennsylvania discovered another kind of oil that came from rocks in the earth. Now there was scarcely a home or shop, even in New Bedford, that still used

3

whale oil in lamps. And then the terrible war between the states had cost New Bedford half its ships.

Until the war, we were almost well to do. Unlike most workers, who lived in boardinghouses with their families, Pa owned a small house. But these days, though Molly was frugal and a clever housekeeper, we could barely make ends meet. Everyone in New Bedford still depended on whaling and the building of ships, but lately there seemed to be more schooners and barks and ships in our harbor than whales left in the sea. No one needed to build more ships, and half the tradesmen were out of work. Men who were valuable to their employers, like my father, were kept on at half pay. Good coopers like Ethan Nye had no work. That's why he left with Pa—so he could earn enough money to marry Rebecca.

Molly finished wringing the sheet out with her hands. "On your parents' wedding day, your father promised your mother he'd never sign on for a voyage again. Your mother, bless her poor departed soul, hated the sea. It claimed her father and both her brothers, and she didn't want it to take her husband, too. A promise made to someone is even holier after they're dead—no good will come of breaking it, lass."

"Listen to you, Molly MacGregor. You're the one who's sounding foolish now." I flicked some water in Molly's face and tried to laugh. "Didn't you tell Rebecca just yesterday that those bad dreams she's been having about the fleet are nonsense?"

"So I did. And so they are." But Molly's face belied her words. She had the kind of look that meant she was having a touch of the "second sight." I have to admit that scared me more than a little.

"Say what you will, girl, your father's old enough to know better. Imagine two girls—young *ladies,* mind you—left for two years or more with no mother to look after you." Molly had come from Scotland over thirty years before, but she still spoke with a faint Scottish burr. Whenever she was upset or excited, her accent thickened. It was near as thick as Scotch broth now.

I was of half a mind to prod her on. But I couldn't risk Molly finding out about me and Caleb Hawke. Old Caleb was the blacksmith down at the shipyards. He had a different idea than most folks of what girls should or shouldn't do with their lives. He reasoned that if a female could labor hard on a farm or work in textile factories in places like Lowell, then a girl with a strong back and the will to match, like me, could work at a forge crafting iron into useful objects. With business slow, he had even let me shape the sharp tip of a harpoon all by myself.

Molly must have read my mind. "And how did you get your clothes so dirty and torn?"

I'm a terrible liar. I was about to 'fess up when I was saved by a peal of laughter from the hallway door.

"Rebecca?" I hadn't expected to see her this morning. She'd awakened with one of her sick headaches. She got them from time to time, more and more often since September, when we heard a rumor that the bark *Oriole* was missing. The *Oriole* had sailed out with the fleet last year, and if she was in trouble, our father and Ethan's ship might be, too.

"You're meant to be in bed," I said. Rebecca just smiled her sweet smile. In the sunshine pouring through the fanlight window, her hair shone like the spun gold in one of the fairy tales that Molly used to tell us. The indigo dress she wore made her look taller and more slender than ever.

"You shouldn't be down here, lassie. You should stay in bed this morning, nursing that headache of yours." Speaking to Rebecca, Molly's voice went soft. My chest tightened. No one's voice ever got soft when they talked to me. Molly, Pa, *everyone* talked gently to my sister. Even me. I was never sure why, except that Rebecca looked as breakable as the porcelain china cups in the parlor cupboard.

Molly wiped her hands on her apron and hurried to Rebecca's side. "You're pale, and your hands are cold as winter," she said, chafing Rebecca's long tapered fingers between her own square, rough hands.

Rebecca laughed off Molly's remarks. "My headache's on the mend. And there's too much to do on washday to lie abed."

"You can't do wash with a headache!" I cried. Along with my father's thick black hair and short stature, I had inherited his sturdy constitution. Rebecca was frail, like our mother.

"Isn't there some mending for me to do, Caitlin?" Rebecca's blue eyes were teasing. "I overheard something on my way downstairs. You tore your petticoat again, lass?" Rebecca had a fine ear for music and mimicked Molly's accent perfectly.

Molly scolded her with a look, then poured boiling water from the kettle into the teapot to heat it. She emptied the hot water into the washtub and spooned some of her headache remedy herb tea into the teapot before filling it again. The fragrance of lavender filled the room.

"Divide the work as you wish," Molly decided.

"What with daily housework and sewing for Rebecca's hope chest, there's enough for everyone."

"Good. Rebecca sews; I scrub." I grinned at Rebecca.

She looked up from pouring tea and returned my smile. "Only if you promise to tell a story while we work."

"It's a fair trade." In our family Pa played the fiddle, and Rebecca sang like a bird and danced with a light foot. But I was proud to be the family's best storyteller.

"Caitlin, you'd better mind the wash while you talk. It's neat and careful housework that stands a girl in good stead, not storytelling," Molly said.

Rebecca added, "Someday you'll thank Molly for making a good housewife out of you."

"When whales come to shore to hand over their oil in kegs," I retorted.

"One of these days you'll set eyes on a fine young man, and love will bowl you over like lightning," Rebecca promised.

For the life of me I couldn't picture myself as a married woman—let alone imagine a man I'd want to wed. If I had to marry, I guessed I'd be a sea captain's wife. I'd sail alongside my husband, raising a family and supervising a crew, as some captains' wives did.

"No letters today?" Rebecca suddenly asked.

I shook my head. "No, not yet." Out of the corner of my eye, I saw her finger her apron pocket. Her thin chest lifted in a quiet sigh. I knew exactly what was in her pocket—the most recent letter from Ethan. It had arrived in New Bedford at the end of August. He had written it in July, when the fleet stopped in

7

Honolulu to take on stores. It was the last anyone had heard from either Pa or Ethan. Rebecca had read that letter so many times that I marveled the ink hadn't been worn clear off it.

Rebecca put aside her tea, then went upstairs to get some thread. I set up the drying rack near the stove and began hanging up the wash.

"I'm going to empty this slop in the yard," Molly said, hoisting the washbucket full of dirty water onto her hip.

I opened the back door for her. Icy air blasted me in the face. It smelled salty, and my spirits lifted. I began to sing an old sea chantey as I refilled the kettle. The song was one my father taught me:

> "I thought I heard the Old Man say,
> Leave Johnny, leave her!
> Go ashore and draw your pay,
> It's time for us to leave her . . ."

I was humming the rest when Molly rushed in. The sight of her face, pale as flour, stopped my heart.

"Where's Rebecca?" she whispered, grabbing my arm.

"Upstairs—"

"Good. Let's spare her if we can. She's going to have enough to deal with if—"

"If . . . ?"

Molly dropped my arm and strode to the coat hooks by the back door. She grabbed the nearest cloak and bundled it around my shoulders. It was her own, and far too big for me. "Take this, lass. Run like the boy you wish you were. *Run!*"

Through the thick, gray wool I could feel Molly's

hands trembling. "Molly!" I half shouted, then gripped her wrists. I searched her dark-blue eyes. "What is wrong? Where am I running?"

"The shipyard—go down to the *Shipping List* news office. . . . I stopped one of the errand boys from Howland's Countinghouse. He was running up the block to tell Mr. Howland that news had come in over the telegraph wires. Something terrible has happened to the Arctic fleet."

I steadied myself on Molly's arm. "Pa's ship? It's lost?"

Molly bit her lip and shook her head in dismay. "I—I don't know, lassie . . ." She started to tousle my hair like she did when I was a child.

I pulled away. "I'm sure it's a mistake. It's another crazy rumor, like the one about the *Oriole*."

Without giving Molly time to answer, I plunged out the back door. Leaves gusted up from the sidewalk. Clutching the woolen cloak with one hand and hitching up my skirt with the other, I pelted down the slate sidewalk. At Libby's Millinery Shop I darted down a backstreet, then worked my way through the maze of narrow alleys that ran behind the shops and boardinghouses right down to the wharves. I usually shunned the alleys, even during the day. New Bedford was full of sailors and drifters, wharf rats who were as likely to slit your throat as grab your purse. Backstreets were no place for a solitary girl. But that morning I could think only about my father, and the shortest way to the waterfront was through the back alleys. I was sure that if I could reach the shipyards fast enough, I could somehow stop the bad news from being true.

Chapter 2

Panting and gasping for breath, I reached the riverfront just as the meetinghouse clock began to chime. The iron gate leading into the smithy's backyard squeaked as I opened it. I picked my way carefully around the mound of scrap iron and neatly stacked cords of wood. I had gone straight to Caleb Hawke's blacksmith shop because Caleb always knew everything there was to know around the wharves. His smithy fronted the Acushnet River and the docks. Glancing out his doorway as he worked at the forge, he had a fine view of the shipyard. People used to joke that Caleb was the real source of all the news in the weekly *Whalemen's Shipping List*.

I opened the heavy back door and inhaled a chestful of hot, smoky air. The windows were closed and shuttered against the weather. Silhouetted by the morning sun, Caleb was in the front door, his back toward me. Past his broad shoulders, I glimpsed a crowd milling around the countinghouses across the way. It was made up mostly of men: seamen, artisans, fishermen, tradesmen, gentlemen in tall hats, dockworkers. Everyone seemed agitated.

"Caleb, what's happening?" I made myself ask.

Caleb turned around. His face was a sea of wrinkles, at the moment deeply creased in a frown. "Word came in early today—the whole Arctic fleet is trapped in the ice."

I wrapped my arms around my chest. "No news about the crews?"

"No news that I know of . . . yet," Caleb answered.

I stared up at him, wishing with all my heart I'd heard wrong. But though his eyes were dark with pity, his chin was set. This disaster wasn't a rumor. Even without knowing the facts, Caleb seemed sure of that.

Well, *I* wasn't. I refused to be. I pulled my cloak around myself and pushed past Caleb. I suddenly hated him. He had no right to give up so easily! "Mr. Gare—he'll tell me more. He probably knows everything already." Henry Gare owned the shipbuilding business where my father had worked until he went back to sea.

"He can't," Caleb warned. "No one knows anything yet. The wire just broke the news about the fleet. The details were sketchy. Maybe more news will arrive before the *Shipping List* comes out tomorrow, or when the Boston or New York papers get in tonight."

I clapped my hands over my ears; I didn't want to hear more. I backed onto the street, right into Mr. Gare.

"Caitlin Jessup!" he cried, catching me by the arms. I whirled to face him. He was a tall, heavyset man, a few years younger than my father, though his hair was thin and showed some gray. He dressed the part of a prosperous businessman with his heavy black cloak and fine hat, but his hands were as calloused as my pa's. His brown eyes were keen and shrewd. Beneath his glance I suddenly realized I looked a frightful mess. My old linsey-woolsey dress was too short, ending way above my boot tops, and the fabric strained against my shoulders. I wore no hat, and my hands were red and chapped.

"I did not think to find you here. I was going to leave word with Caleb—" He stopped and searched my face. He saw I had already heard so, clearing his throat, he went on. "Then I was headed straight for your house. There is terrible news, but there is also hope."

He steered me back into Caleb's shop and closed the door behind us. He motioned for Caleb to light one of the swinging metal lamps above his workbench. Then he opened his cloak and pulled a newspaper out of his pocket.

"Is that from San Francisco?" I eyed it greedily.

He shook his head. "One of my agents brought this up from New York. He got here only minutes ago. It's today's *Times*." He opened it. It was dated November 6, 1871. Mr. Gare's finger pointed to a column on the far right. A headline read "Disasters at Sea." For a moment the words below seem to swim before my eyes, but I forced myself to skim the first paragraph, which spoke first of a shipwreck and then went on: ". . . He also reports a terrible disaster to the Arctic whaling fleet; caught in the ice, thirty-three vessels were lost or abandoned. . . ."

"Caitlin." Mr. Gare put his arm around my shoulder. "Read on . . . it lists the vessels which are safe and the captains who survived."

"And my father—"

"Neither he nor the *Priscilla* are mentioned. But don't lose hope. There is very little information. In a few days, or at least by next week, we will hear more. It is a good sign that so many have survived."

"So there really is hope." Caleb voiced my own thoughts.

"More than hope. I am sure that men were not left on the ice to perish."

Caleb and Mr. Gare discussed the possible fate of the fleet and the ships themselves—and the terrible loss to New Bedford. The best of our fleet had sailed a year ago on this voyage. Every bank and counting-house would be involved in the loss. Some ships had escaped outside the ice before it froze solid, but others had been crushed in the ice. Many of our home port vessels were listed among the abandoned ships.

But I only half listened to the men. By the flickering lamplight I read and reread the article. Mr. Gare was right; there was good cause to believe my father and Ethan were fine. Still, I wondered how in the world I would break the news to Rebecca. And I felt uneasy in my heart. Her dreams of late had been of Pa and Ethan drowning.

"Now let me take you home," Mr. Gare said, carefully folding up the paper and tucking it back under his cloak.

I was about to protest that I could make it home on my own, but actually I felt chilled and frightened. I would be glad of Mr. Gare's company. We said good-bye to Caleb and headed out the front door. Mr. Gare turned up Water Street, away from the docks. "I would have taken my carriage, but the streets are so crowded," he said.

"The walk will do me good," I told him.

He offered me his arm, and I felt awkward taking it. Still, the shock had made me unsteady on my feet, somehow. Half my mind was trying to figure out what words to say to Rebecca.

We walked down North Water Street to Williams Street, then passed Liberty Hall, where John Fielding was putting up showcards for the next musical feature, a brass band from Boston. As we waited on a corner for a knot of carriages and ice wagons to pass, Henry Gare patted my hand. "I promised your father, Caitlin, I would look after you girls while he was gone."

"You have certainly done that," I said. "And more. We have not wanted for food or fuel in all the months since he left."

"It was agreed I would do that, and he would repay me as part of his lay. The take in a voyage like this promised to be considerable." He did not add that there would be no lay now. My father would probably come back ruined. If, I couldn't help thinking, he came back at all.

"But that is not all I promised," Mr. Gare went on. He paused long enough to guide me across the street to the sidewalk in front of Milford's General Store and Provisions.

"Look at me, Caitlin," he said, making me stop right in front of the shop. "I promised your father that should he meet with misfortune, I would be sure you girls would not be in want. I promised him you will be taken care of as long as needed, in the manner to which you are accustomed."

I felt my eyes well with tears. "I cannot talk of my father as being dead. He will be fine; he will live through this. We Jessups have always found a way to manage." Then, not wanting to seem ungrateful, I quickly added, "But I feel—and I know Rebecca feels—grateful for everything you have done for us."

"And will do—until your father returns."

We walked in silence up the sloping street and finally stopped in front of our small house. The chestnut tree in the yard was bare, but the young oak was full of brown leaves that rattled in the wind. They made me think of death and ghosts, and I shivered slightly before opening the gate.

"Caitlin, let me come in with you."

"No, Mr. Gare. I am truly grateful, but I must tell Rebecca and Molly myself," I said.

"I will bring the paper round first thing tomorrow. Though I doubt there will be much more news than this. At least there's hope, Caitlin. All—and everyone—was not lost."

We said our farewells, and I walked into the house. Down the short front hall that led to the kitchen, I could see Rebecca sewing by the stove. Her expression was peaceful and dreamy. Clearly, Molly hadn't told her a thing. I closed the door behind me and hung Molly's cloak on the rack near the foot of the stairs.

"Caitlin?" Rebecca looked up sharply. "Where have you been?"

"To the shipyard."

I walked past Rebecca before casting a pleading glance at Molly, who had taken over my post at the washtub. Then I squared my shoulders and stooped down in front of Rebecca. I took the sock she was darning out of her hands. "There's been some news—"

"Of Ethan—and Father?" Rebecca's face lit up. "Is there a letter?" She looked at my hands, red from the wind.

"Where are your gloves? . . ." She started to admonish me, but some sixth sense stopped her. She gazed at my bare head, my old dress. "You went to the docks like that?"

Molly gripped the top of Rebecca's chair so hard I thought the wood would break.

"The Arctic fleet—all of it, not just the ships from New Bedford—has foundered on the ice. But the crews, some at least, have been saved. There's no list yet—not of the crew members." I blurted it all out in a single breath.

I heard Rebecca's cry. And Molly's sob. The room went a bit fuzzy, and the last thing I remember was that everything seemed to tilt and swirl.

Chapter 3

The morning after I fainted for the first time in my life, I woke in my own bed from a dream about my father. In the dream he had been downstairs in our kitchen. Clear as clear I could hear him singing as he stoked the stove and pumped water into the tea kettle. I had snuggled deeper under the quilt and started to smile before I realized it was only a dream. I might never see my father again. I kept my eyes closed and tried to remember the exact sound of his voice.

"Are you awake?" Rebecca's voice jarred me.

I rolled over in the four-poster bed we shared and saw she was already up. I sat up and rubbed my eyes. The kerosene lamp on the dresser bathed the room in soft light. Through the curtains the sky was still dark. The sounds in the kitchen were made by Molly poking the fire to life in the stove and making breakfast. Molly . . . *not* my father.

"Caitlin? You're crying?"

I threw myself down, my back to her, and buried my face in the pillow. It had been years since I had cried in front of anyone—maybe since I had cried at all. Rebecca sat next to me on the bed and smoothed my hair. Dressed only in her chemise and petticoat, she was shivering so hard I could actually hear her teeth chatter. Unless we were sick, we never slept with a fire in the bedroom hearth.

"Poor Caitlin, it's all right to cry. You don't always have to be the brave one," she soothed, her own voice breaking.

I sat up then and threw my arms around her neck and wept like a spring river in flood time. She sobbed, too. Hugging each other tightly, we rocked back and forth, sharing the same pain, the same fears, as if we were two sides of a single person.

"What will we do without Pa?" I cried over and over.

But Rebecca couldn't answer. She wasn't worried only about Pa. After Ethan asked her to marry him, she told me that she was sure she would die if she ever had to live without him. Remembering that, I pulled myself together.

"Now aren't we being silly," I said, stifling a new round of tears. I leaned back from Rebecca and tried to force a smile. "We both look a fright, and Henry Gare is coming within the hour." I rubbed the sleeve of my flannel nightgown against my face and dabbed Rebecca's tear-streaked cheeks with the sheet. She managed to smile back, then reached for a handkerchief and blew her nose.

"We're acting like the news is all bad—but it isn't." I tried to put a brave face on it. "Mr. Gare will come with the paper in a little while, and we'll see Ethan and Pa are listed among the crewmen saved."

Rebecca nodded and went over to the washstand. While I wriggled into the scratchy wool underdrawers Molly insisted we wear under our cotton bloomers, Rebecca poked a hole in the thin ice that had formed in the washbasin overnight. She splashed the cold water on her cheeks and eyes. When she looked up I met her glance in the mirror, and this time she managed a stronger smile. Then she put on her old dove-gray silk and wool dress, the one she saved for second best. She gave me one last hug and then went down to the kitchen.

I washed as fast as I could and practically leaped into my clothes. I was embarrassed at how shabby I had looked the day before, so I was careful to choose my only decent weekday dress, a maroon tartan plaid. I stared at myself in the oval standing mirror as I did up the bodice of my dress. The circles under *my* eyes today were as bad as Rebecca's, and my head ached from crying.

All too clearly I remembered my last conversation with my father. We had gone down to the docks on a bright November day a year ago. While Rebecca bid farewell to Ethan, Pa drew me aside, out of the bustle and commotion of the crowd gathered to see the *Priscilla* and several other ships set sail.

"Caitlin, my girl. You are braver than Rebecca, and stronger in some ways. With Ethan and myself gone, be sure to take care of her. And you can learn from her the gentler things, so let her teach you," he told me.

When I groaned at that he brushed back my hair, which I still wore loose. It was a hopeless tangle of curls in the harbor wind. "I mean that, Caitlin. But if—if we don't come back as soon as we plan—you will take care of her."

Now I wondered if he'd had a premonition we might not see him again. The thought was so horrible that I almost started crying again. "Caitlin Jessup, stop acting foolish," I told my reflection in the mirror. I yanked the brush through my hair a few more times, then rushed down the steps. I had only started wearing my hair up a month ago, when I turned sixteen, and I wasn't very good at putting it up yet. Rebecca could fix it for me in front of the kitchen stove.

"There's good news and bad," said Henry Gare an hour later. He handed his hat and greatcoat to Molly at the door, walked into the parlor, and reached for Rebecca's hands. Then he caught my glance over her shoulder and gave me a quick smile. My heart, which had been beating fast as a hummingbird's wings, slowed down.

"Mr. Gare, you're cold as ice, and you'll catch a chill." Rebecca, always the gracious one, led him to the stove. She tried to settle him in a chair, but he chose to stand, warming his hands over the stove.

"The good news first," he said. "Not one person has perished."

"Thank God. I knew the good Lord would not let these bonnie lasses come to such grief," Molly cried.

I watched Mr. Gare. His expression was not exactly relieved—if everyone was saved, why didn't he look happier?

"But what's the bad news, then?" I asked.

Rebecca cast me a pleading look. She so wanted

to savor this moment. "Let Mr. Gare tell us how he knows no one perished."

Mr. Gare held my glance. "The bad news is that there is no final list yet of the men who were saved. Some of the captains are listed, and the masters and first mates. But nearly a third of the twelve hundred or so men who sailed with the fleet are not listed. It appears that some boats, not yet caught in the ice when it began to freeze over mid-September, took on all the provisions and crewmen that they could carry from the icebound ships. It must have been a slow and trying voyage back down to Honolulu. But I haven't got more information than that."

"But that's not bad news," I said, unable to keep from smiling. "It's just news delayed."

"And surely the *Shipping List* will have more information next week," Rebecca stated.

Mr. Gare nodded. "My brother, Jeremiah, is leaving tomorrow on the railroad for San Francisco to see what he can learn firsthand from our agent there. The trip should take a little over a week, and he will wire us as soon as he hears anything. I have told him particularly to look out for your father's name and for Ethan's. He might actually find them as ships from Honolulu come into port."

Then we all talked awhile about what the loss of the fleet might mean to New Bedford. By the time Mr. Gare left our house that morning our grief was lessened, though our mood stayed somber.

A week more passed before the complete list of captains and crews rescued and brought to San Francisco or Honolulu was published. You can imagine our joy to find both Ethan's and our father's names there. The day our worries ended, our wait began for letters—blessed, newsy, wonderful letters. Every morning we were barely able to sit through breakfast, waiting for the first mail. But nothing arrived.

Thanksgiving came and went, and there were still no letters. By mid-December, though no one spoke of it, we were all sure something had gone terribly wrong. There were still no letters, and other men had begun to come home. While the newspapers ran articles about the financial losses to the fleet, we kept searching for news of some mishap to survivors.

Many evenings—more so as time passed—Mr. Gare came to our house after dinner, or even occasionally to dine. He was always a great help. As single women we weren't free to scour the various boardinghouses, taverns, and seamen's lodgings down by the docks. Almost every day he checked them himself to talk with the returning whalemen. But no one from the *Priscilla* turned up in New Bedford.

By Christmas we were too downcast to feel like celebrating, but Mr. Gare refused to let us give up hope. Christmas Eve he turned up with a tree and a king's ransom's worth of spermaceti candles—made from the clearest of whale oil, and very, very dear.

"In case they come home Christmas Eve, the house should be full of light and song," he told us. And so our parlor was bright and we were all gathered around Rebecca's piano, singing "Deck the Halls," when the knock we had been listening for came at the door.

Chapter 4

I jumped up while everyone was still singing and threw open the door. A man stood on the top step. He wore a heavy wool seaman's jacket, and in his right hand he held a dark-blue cap. His beard was so thick and grizzled that I couldn't make out his face. But his eyes were pure blue, and he had my father's height and build.

"Pa!" I shouted. I was about to throw my arms around him when the smell of rum on his breath stopped me. My cheeks burned. How could I have imagined this drunken seaman was my father!

"Father?" Rebecca was just behind me.

"No, ma'am. I'm looking for the daughters of Jonathan Jessup, Miss Rebecca and Miss Caitlin." He had a Boston accent, and his voice shook from the cold or drink, I knew not which.

Mr. Gare took charge. "I think our visitor needs strong coffee and food. Maybe he has some long-awaited news."

I saw that under his beard the man's cheeks were

sunken, and he was very thin. Mr. Gare guided the stranger into the parlor.

"I don't rightly know if I should stay." He looked from Rebecca to me, then back at Mr. Gare. "I really should just say my piece and leave." He struggled to continue. "You are all so happy here, and my news is so terrible. I cannot stay." He made as if to go to the door.

My heart stopped. Rebecca pulled me close to her, and we stood near the piano, our arms locked together.

Mr. Gare blocked his way. "Out with it, Mr. . . ."

"Bailey, Jethro Bailey." He pulled out a ragged bandanna and mopped his brow. "I knew them both, Jonathan and young Ethan—"

"Knew?" Henry Gare positioned himself near Rebecca. I kept my eyes on Mr. Bailey. "From the *Priscilla*?"

"No. Can't say I've ever seen that vessel, though Jonathan spoke proud of her."

"I don't understand," Rebecca finally said, her voice quiet and remarkably steady. "How do you know my father and Ethan if you didn't sail with them?"

"Sail with them I did . . . after they left Honolulu. I was the first mate on the ship *Dorset*."

"That's an English vessel," Mr. Gare interjected. "The *Shipping List* mentioned when it embarked for San Francisco, but there's been no news of her for some time now."

"We left Honolulu mid-November," Jethro Bailey said. "Aboard were Ethan Nye and Jonathan Jessup. I don't know what boat brought them to Honolulu from the Arctic, but I do know Ethan had the fever when they landed in Honolulu. Since he was too sick to set sail with the others, he and Jonathan stayed behind. He mended quick enough, I guess. When we left Honolulu, he was in good health.''

As he spoke, the man stared mainly at his feet. "The weather was mild at first, and with the wind at our back we thought we would make San Francisco in good time. But we ran into a terrible hurricane. Men went overboard and were never seen again—Ethan among them. When the ship broke up, most of the crew was lost. I was in a lifeboat with your father, but we capsized in the waves not a day after the *Dorset* went down. I never saw him or our other mates again.''

Rebecca dug her fingers in my wrist. "Ethan's drowned?''

"My father's drowned?'' I heard myself ask the question, but I felt like my mouth belonged to someone else. Mr. Gare put his hand on my shoulder. I lowered myself into a chair.

"Oh, miss, yes. I tied myself to a spar and drifted for a day before I was picked up by a ship heading for Oregon. I have come from there, direct to here, as I promised your father I would if ill befell him.''

Rebecca was whiter than snow. But she surprised us all by standing up straight and tall. "Ethan will never be back.'' Her voice quavered only slightly. She walked over to the grimy seaman and took his calloused hand. "Then tell us, tell *me,* everything you remember about him and our father those last days of their lives.''

"No!'' I cried. "I don't believe you!'' I

25

turned to Rebecca. "And you shouldn't, either. This man is drunk and will make up anything for a hot meal." I practically spit the words out. "I would know if Pa were dead; I'd feel it inside. He's alive. Alive!" I sobbed, and broke free of Molly's grip.

"Caitlin, come back here!" Molly cried after me. But I was already halfway up the stairs. I ran into my father's room and slammed the door shut and locked it. I stood with my back pressed against the door, as if I could press out the horror. "He's wrong, he's wrong, Pa. I know it," I moaned.

"Caitlin, open the door!" Rebecca cried from outside. But I didn't want my sister. I only wanted my father. Suddenly I felt as if one of Caleb's irons, red from the forge, had branded my heart. I prayed that I might at that very moment just die. But my heart beat stubborn and strong in my chest. I burst into tears and staggered across the room. I threw myself across the bed and wept until my throat was raw and my eyes felt on fire. After a long while, it seemed my soul was cried dry.

I do not remember the next few days. I barricaded myself in my father's room right through Christmas and Christmas night. The noise of the house went on below. Almost every hour, Rebecca would talk to me softly through the door. I only told her to go away— and then I stopped talking to her all together. It was a terrible thing, I think, to hold myself so separate from Rebecca. But I couldn't help it.

Molly had Dr. Brownwell come over, but I would not open the door to him. Molly told him I was too stubborn to do real harm to myself. She said it loud enough that I heard her through the door. I wanted to prove her wrong. I felt like an open wound. I thought the soul of me would just drain away and I'd be with my father again. If I stayed there long enough, curled up on the bed, I might just starve to death.

Chapter 5

But I survived. Maybe because I was a pig-headed Jessup, still too much my father's daughter to give up. The day after Christmas, I unlocked the door. I closed it behind me and crossed the hall to my room. The clean, cold air revived me some, though I was weak and lightheaded. I peeled off my Christmas Eve finery, put on my dressing gown, and combed the knots out of my hair with my fingers. I longed to bathe away my grief as well as the grime of three days without washing. My stomach felt so hollow it hurt, and I wondered if I could ever eat again. Next breath all I wanted to do was eat. The smell of Molly's cooking drifted up the steps and enticed me to the kitchen.

Molly looked up. "You need a bath, lass," she said. Her tone was neither gentle nor harsh, but she looked relieved. She was matter-of-fact, as though I had gone for a trip to relatives down in Boston and had just come back. I had been gone someplace and I was back. Plain as that. She handed me one of the precious oranges Mr. Gare had brought Christmas

Eve. I peeled it with shaky fingers. The juice burst sweet and fresh in my dry mouth. I tried to eat the rest slowly to make it last, but I devoured it in two or three bites.

Molly set up a little screen in front of the wooden tub, which she filled with water from the stove. I climbed in and sank to my chin in suds.

"May I wash your hair?" Rebecca's voice stopped my heart. How could I face her? I had let her down at the most difficult time of our lives. I felt like a coward. I had broken my last promise to my father. I hadn't been there to take care of her.

"Becca . . ." I forced myself to look up. She was tying an apron over her black skirt. Dressed in mourning, she looked paler than usual, but her expression was peaceful and composed. I think finally knowing what had become of Ethan had somehow calmed her. Still, the soft light that usually lit her face seemed to have been snuffed out. I wanted to explain myself, but I really had no idea why I had acted as I did.

Rebecca put her finger on my lips and just smiled. She took a pitcher of warm water and forced my head back gently. As she massaged the soap into my head, she said, "There's nothing to explain, Caitlin. Pa did the same thing when Mama died. He locked himself up for days in the shed. He came out in his own good time. It was a while after that before he could play his fiddle or sing again. But he did. He went on. And you're like him; Molly always says that."

A few days later, we attended a church service for Pa and Ethan. The heavy black mourning dress that

Molly had conjured up from somewhere stifled me. Back home, I still felt smothered after I changed to a simple black skirt. I wondered if my pa would have liked his daughters wearing such somber clothes. But part of me had gone numb.

That night Molly put an extra board in the table and set it with our best china. The stream of towns-people expressing condolences and bringing food slowly dwindled, until we were left with just Mr. Gare.

"This is a difficult day for you girls," he said. "But we have to discuss your future."

We sat silently, and Mr. Gare continued. "To take this voyage, your father had to mortgage the house. He planned to use his cut of the lay to pay the debt." He paused and looked down at his hands. When he looked up, his face was troubled. "I will be sure you want for nothing, as I promised your father. In the event of his death, he named me your official guard-ian until Rebecca turns twenty-one. But," he added, turning to Rebecca and myself, "I'm afraid the house will have to be sold. Perhaps we can wait a few months, until the panic in town settles down. We will get a better price then. Meanwhile I can carry the mortgage—"

"We'll have to move?" I looked around the living room, and my eyes settled on the miniature of Mama. Suddenly I, who had so longed for freedom and ad-venture, wished I could turn into a tree or a mountain and never be unearthed from this place.

"Where will we go?" Rebecca cried.

"You could live with me and my sisters," Mr. Gare suggested. Then he cleared his throat and reached into his vest pocket. "And there is another possibility." Something in his voice made my heart stop. He pulled out a telegram. "This came the other day from New York. It is from your Aunt Felicity and Uncle Isaiah. They'd be willing to take you in."

"They didn't even come to the church service!" Rebecca said.

"No." Mr. Gare didn't have to say more. My mother's brother and his wife had disdained my father. They hadn't spoken to our family since my parents wed, twenty-two years ago.

"My father would never have wanted us to go to New York and live with them," said Rebecca with great dignity.

"They are wealthy, child," Mr. Gare reminded her. "They can give you both a comfortable life and promising future."

Molly just humphed. But Rebecca's blue eyes grew steely. "We have time to think about our future, and perhaps we will come and live with you when the house is sold. Until then, I would like to stay on here. But my father appointed you, Mr. Gare, not Felicity or Isaiah, to be our guardian. We will not go to them."

In spite of my grief, I almost cheered.

The next few months blurred by for me. Rebecca and I talked often of what our future might be. First she suggested we get jobs at one of the new textile mills in town. Perhaps between our wages and rent from a boarder, we could stay on in the house with Molly to help. I laughed that idea down. Rebecca wasn't sturdy enough for mill work, and I thought I would die being cooped in a factory all day long.

Then I proposed we take the money left after selling the house and run a boardinghouse. Rebecca and Molly seriously considered it, though I was told I'd have to contribute to the formidable housekeeping tasks. I swore I was up to it. This time, Mr. Gare got wind of our plans. He showed us there would be almost no money left when the house was sold and the mortgage paid.

Rebecca, strangely enough, didn't seem disheartened. Had I been more myself, I might have noticed she had begun to read the newspaper and study maps. Some plan was brewing inside her head, but I was too depressed to try to ferret out what she was up to. Later I remembered how she began waiting eagerly every day for the mail just around that time. Now I think I must have been half blind.

One Saturday afternoon when she had gone to the parlor to write some letters, Mr. Gare came calling. It was a mild day in late March. I was in our small garden, getting some air.

"Caitlin, good day." Mr. Gare tipped his hat. "Is Rebecca in?"

"Yes." I started for the door. "Would you like tea?"

"No—no, not now. I thought, perhaps, you might enjoy a little walk." He seemed preoccupied.

"That would be nice," I replied. The taste of spring in the air made me want to stretch my legs. "I'll get my bonnet and see if Rebecca wants to join us—"

"I thought just the two of us could walk downtown."

We strolled down Middle Street, peering in the shops. It wasn't until we rounded the corner of North

Street, and the tall masts of the ships came into view over the roofs of the houses, that I realized I hadn't been down to the water since the news of Pa's death. I, who had always loved the sea more than anything, suddenly hated the sight of the ships, the lighthouse, and most of all, the deadly ocean.

"Caitlin." Something in Mr. Gare's voice made me turn to face him. "I know this has been a difficult time for you and Rebecca, but I need to ask you something."

For the first time since I'd known him, he looked unsure of himself. The wind gusted up from the river, and my hair had worked loose from beneath my hat. I held it back from my face as he flashed a quick, nervous smile. "Caitlin, you know I am not a young man. Your father was forty when he died, and I am nearly that, but I am healthy and strong, and my family lives to a good old age."

He guided me around the corner, to a spot where we were sheltered from the wind. "I have never married. I have been too busy with business and, to be honest, I have not found a woman with spirit enough to please me."

Rebecca, he wants to ask me if he might ask Rebecca to wed him without offending her. He wants to know if it's too soon.

I was thinking that when he put his hand under my chin. "Caitlin, I think we could be happy together. I can provide handsomely for you and your sister, and I think in time you could learn to care for me, the way I have grown to care for you."

"Me?" I practically shrieked with surprise. Some passersby turned their heads. I felt my cheeks grow

hot. I dropped my voice, but couldn't meet his eyes. "You want *me* to marry you?"

He let out a sigh. I quickly took his hand. "Mr. Gare—"

"You could call me—"

"Mr. Gare," I repeated with emphasis. "You have been the best of friends to me and my sister. Just now I thought you were going to ask me if you thought you might be able to wed Rebecca—if she were enough over Ethan to consider a proposal from you. But me? Married?"

"You are young, I know. I could wait a year or two. But that would help us both get used to the idea, and it would stop the talk in town—"

"Talk?" I looked up quickly. The concern in his face was all too real.

"It is not altogether appropriate for me to keep helping you financially, though I don't care what any of these busybodies think. But still, it is not good for girls your age to be without a man's legal as well as moral protection."

I forced myself to listen. It made sense, after all. And he was a good man. Yet. Stealing a glance at him, my heart sank. He was a friend, almost a father, perhaps even an older brother—but not a man to love. Still, I had Rebecca to consider. And our future. "I will think about it, Mr. Gare," I said sincerely. "But I don't see why you don't ask Rebecca."

"Because I don't lo— care for her in the same way, Caitlin. She is a lovely woman, but I need strength and spirit in the partner I choose to spend my life with."

"Rebecca's stronger than any of us thought."

He nodded gravely. "That she's been lately." He

didn't say more about my sister. "You will consider my proposal, then. However long you must think about it, I don't mind. But plans for your life must be made soon."

We walked back up the hill toward my house. My mind was a jumble of thoughts. Mr. Gare was careful to talk about pleasant, neutral things—the spring planting further inland, the weather here. But when he offered, I did not take his arm.

Chapter 6

"**M**arry Henry Gare!" Rebecca dropped down into a chair. I had left Mr. Gare and walked right into the kitchen to make my announcement.

For once Molly was speechless. She stood with her wooden ladle in the air, just staring at me as I untied my bonnet. I had expected surprise, but not quite this. I wasn't sure whether to laugh or be insulted. "Is someone asking me to marry such an outlandish idea?" I demanded.

Rebecca smiled the first real smile I'd seen on her face in months. "Caitlin Jessup, any man would be lucky to marry you. But truly, you haven't given even the slightest thought to marriage before now. You've not even mentioned liking any boy—or man—let alone love. Last I heard you never wanted to marry!"

"Marry at your age? And marry a man your father's age!" Molly found her voice again. She put the ladle back into the fish chowder. "Has grief driven you out of your mind, lass? He is too old for you, and too—too—"

"Too good?" I suggested, folding my arms across my chest. When I made my announcement, I hadn't the smallest inclination to marry Mr. Gare. Now some contrary streak in my nature reveled in the idea.

"No, he's just a good friend. He has been so kind to us, but we cannot take advantage of him this way," Rebecca said.

"Marry Henry Gare!" Molly cried. "Over my dead body!"

"I don't know what you have to say about it—"

Molly plunged on past my protest. "You, Caitlin Jessup, are a strong-willed girl with a mind and heart of your own. You will marry for love or nothing. Otherwise you won't just make your own life miserable—you'll be the death of any man that isn't the heart and soul of you. I won't have you killing off kind old Mr. Gare."

"He's not that old," I retorted. "Isn't he your age?" Molly looked hurt.

"Don't be impertinent!" Rebecca said sharply.

I touched Molly's sleeve. "Oh Molly, don't mind me and don't look so upset. I don't *want* to marry him, but it would be a help, wouldn't it—solving all our problems."

"It would only make both your lives miserable in the end," Rebecca said, sounding wise.

Molly opened the firebox on the stove and stoked the fire with a poker. Then, sounding distant, she said, "It would be a great mistake, but I cannot tell you what to do."

Rebecca broke in. "Nor will you have to. Caitlin will not marry this man. It's not fair, and she's too young for marriage." Rebecca looked down at her smooth, white hands. "Besides, I think I may have found the perfect solution to our problems."

Molly cocked her head and cast a suspicious glance in my direction. I shrugged. Whatever Rebecca had up her sleeve, I knew nothing of it.

"But," Rebecca added, "my plan's not ripe enough to talk about just yet."

Though Rebecca had offered to go with me when I told Mr. Gare my decision, I had reasons for going alone. The next morning I hurried through the fog to the business office of his shipbuilding company. As I waited to see him, I paced nervously.

Finally he came up behind me. "Caitlin?"

I turned to face him, taking a deep breath. "I've made my decision."

"Let's not talk here." Mr. Gare went for his cloak and gave an instruction to the clerk. Then he guided me through the maze of vendors and food stalls, down Purchase Street to Tilden's Confectionery Shop. We sat at one of the small tables with a view of the street. He ordered us both hot chocolate and sweet rolls.

"I expected you to take longer to decide." He sat back in his chair.

I met his eyes and, oh, at that moment they looked so kind that I was tempted to change my mind. Perhaps a girl could learn to love a man who was just a friend. But I remembered how Rebecca had told me not so long ago that someday love would come and knock me over like lightning. Mr. Gare didn't kindle the faintest spark.

"I appreciate your offer, Mr. Gare," I said, staring into my chocolate. "But I cannot accept."

I made myself look him in the eye again. He

shifted his glance from me down to the table. "I suspected that—but you do understand I wasn't asking you out of pity, or just practicality, or just to help you and Rebecca."

It hurt me to be truthful. But I owed him that. "I understand. And I wish I could care for you differently. You have been such a friend to us." Then I worked up my nerve and asked him one last time, "You will not consider Rebecca?"

"I doubt she'd have me, either," he said quickly. "Even so, she is not the woman I would like to marry."

And then, with a grace I have never forgotten to this day, he changed the subject. It seemed the insurance money had just come in, and the settlement was more generous than expected. We would have a small nest egg that might help us find a better situation after we sold the house and paid off the mortgage.

On the first of April, Rebecca broke her big news. She waited until Molly was off to market, then drew me into the parlor and sat me down in the rocker. She sat on the crewel-covered stool at my feet and spread her skirts around her.

"I have news, Caitlin. A plan for our future."

"Oh, your news is ripe for picking, is it?" I teased, then caught my breath. Beneath the quiet surface of her face, she looked like a well about to bubble over. I watched on edge as she fished a packet of letters out of her pocket. They were tied up with one of her blue hair ribbons, and the envelopes were addressed in a bold, clear hand. She held the packet in her hands. It was a moment more before she went on.

"Yes. My news is ready for telling now—and everything is working out better than in my wildest dreams. Caitlin, do you remember Emma Everett?"

I stopped rocking in my chair and nodded. "The Cortlands' servant girl." I racked my brains for a moment. Emma had attended the same church as us. She was a pleasant young woman who would have been pretty if not for her pockmarked face. "What in the world does Emma Everett have to do with us?"

"Remember how she went West?"

"Right!" I clapped my hands together. "How *could* I forget?" Emma's departure from our circle of acquaintances in New Bedford had created quite a stir, though for the life of me I couldn't recall the details.

"She answered an ad in the *Sentinel*," Rebecca prompted.

"To be a housekeeper?"

Rebecca took a deep breath. "To be a wife."

"To someone she'd never met?" I asked, but suddenly the small scandal Emma caused came rushing back to me. There had been some cruel talk about how a girl as homely as Emma needed to answer a stranger's ad to find a man willing to marry her. I hadn't paid attention to the marrying part at the time. I just thought it was terribly exciting to set out on a new life out West, where land was cheap and plentiful, and gold filled the hills and streams.

"Well, I saw such an ad, quite by accident, about two months ago," Rebecca went on. "And I decided to answer it."

I gaped at Rebecca. "You answered an advertisement? In the newspaper? To wed a stranger?" I jumped up, nearly upsetting the rocking chair.

"Someone we don't know? Who isn't from New Bedford? After you wouldn't let me wed Henry Gare, you are going to marry a perfect stranger? Have you lost your mind, Rebecca?"

Rebecca looked up at me a moment, then shook her head. "It's not the same thing as Henry Gare and you."

I scoffed. "It certainly isn't! We know him. He is a friend. Our father trusted him enough to make him our guardian. . . . He won't let you do this. I'm sure he won't."

"He won't have a choice. He was our guardian only until I came of age. I am now twenty-one."

I put my hands to my face. Of course. Rebecca's birthday last month had been nearly forgotten in all our grief. I stared down at her and shook my head in disbelief.

Rebecca got up and went to the window. Leaning against the pane, she looked out at the brown yard with its patches of old snow and fresh purple crocuses.

"How, after Ethan, could you marry someone you have never met, let alone don't love?" I demanded.

Rebecca's shoulders stiffened. She faced me. "Caitlin. About Ethan. I have known a most wonderful love, and I will never be able to love a man that way again. But I am young, and I want to wed, and I think I can fashion a new life for us."

"Us?"

"I would like you to come with me out West, to Nebraska."

"To live with you and this man you have not even met? In Nebraska?" My dreams of the West had more to do with Colorado mining towns or the hills

41

of Oregon. All I knew about Nebraska was that the transcontinental railroad went clear across it, through Omaha. It did not sound like someplace I would like to live—let alone Rebecca.

"No, I haven't met him in person," she said. "There's no chance to. He cannot leave his homestead to come here. But we have exchanged letters, and I think I will like him, and maybe even grow to love him. I don't know that. If we meet and feel we aren't fit for each other, then I will either come back here or perhaps move to Omaha or San Francisco."

I couldn't believe it was my quiet sister speaking. I didn't even know how to argue with her about this. Rebecca leave New Bedford? Except for the marrying part, answering an ad to move to the frontier sounded like something I might do, but not Rebecca!

"You don't even know what he looks like," I pointed out.

Rebecca bit her lip and blushed slightly. "Oh, yes I do. It is not a good likeness; the image is blurred. But here—" She picked up the bundle of letters she had put on the carpet and pulled a small daguerreotype from an envelope. It showed three roughly dressed men leaning on picks and shovels beside some railroad tracks. One wore a Union uniform from the war. The image was blurred, as Rebecca said, but they were all smiling and seemed so eager, so confident, as if no hardship were big enough to touch them. Rebecca shyly pointed to one of the men. He wore no uniform and was taller than the others.

"That's him," she said. "That's Nathaniel Briscomb. He calls himself Nate."

◕◠◕

Chapter 7

"Read me Nate's letter again, Caitlin. The last one," said Rebecca as the train chugged down the tracks somewhere between the Mississippi and Missouri Rivers. It was a scorching hot afternoon in the middle of June, and we were halfway to Nebraska and our new life with Nate Briscomb.

I rummaged in a carpetbag and located the letter. We had left our mourning clothes behind in New Bedford, and Rebecca now sat opposite me in a dark plum traveling dress. She had taken off her gloves and was dabbing at her forehead with a handkerchief scented with lavender water. Beneath the grime of the journey, her face was pale.

"My head hurts so, and the light is too bright and the sun so hot, even with the shades drawn," she said, closing her eyes. Each bump of the wheels on the track made her wince.

I watched, helpless. The trip from New York to Omaha, Nebraska, where we would change trains for Lincoln, was far from over. We weren't even due into Omaha until early the next morning. At Henry

43

Gare's insistence we had bought tickets for the ladies car, but though we were spared the attentions of unpleasant male travelers, the seats were no more comfortable than those in the regular passenger cars.

To soothe Rebecca, and to get my own mind off the uncertain future we faced, I read aloud:

Sweetgrass, Nebraska
May 20, 1872

Dear Rebecca,

I have made arrangements for your arrival. I will meet you in Lincoln on June 17. The train is due in from Omaha—if no trouble comes up—about 3 P.M. That should give us enough time to make it back to Sweetgrass about 8. You will see the house for the first time at sunset.

You asked me to tell you a little more about myself and how I came to homestead here. As I told you I have no family to speak of, though a couple outside of St. Joes adopted me from an orphanage when I was 10. They were kind people and undertook my education.

I was a boy of 15 at the end of the war, at which time I saw an ad for railroad workers in a paper. I signed on with a Union Pacific agent. I was foreman of a crew at Promontory Point in 1869 when we met the Central Pacific, the last spikes were driven, and the transcontinental railroad was born. The tintype I sent you was taken a few weeks before that with some of the other men in my outfit. They went on to California, Oregon, and Colorado, but I missed farming and had a hankering after some land. The

*Union Pacific was granting cheap land in Ne-
braska for men who had worked the rails. I
decided to stake my claim near Sweetgrass. The
future is big here for those with the heart for
it, and the land begins to love you back if you
are patient with it—and willing to work.*

*It is a hard life I live, and a lonely one.
Though I hope with you to change that. But I
love this place. The space here makes a person
bigger than themselves, if you know what I
mean.*

*And, yes, I was serious about your sister
being welcome here. Not only will she be good
company for you, but we can use the help. And
when she is older, and ready for a husband, I
know she will have the pick of the finest men
around here. There are many good, honest souls
who are eager to start families of their own.*

*I hope you will learn to love it here as I do.
I cannot wait until I get to see you.*

> *Until then, I remain,*
> *Respectfully,*
> *Nathaniel Briscomb (Nate)*

I looked up and saw Rebecca had dozed off. I sat
quietly watching the scenery go by. Tall clouds towered over the western horizon, and I thought tomorrow might not be as fair as today. The train rolled
through acres of farmland. Small, homey houses and
proud red barns passed by our window, and farmers
looked up from their work to wave. Neat, squared-
off fields of corn stretched as far as the eye could
see, and the sun hung low over the horizon, casting

a warm pink light on everything. There were not many trees, and the further west we went the flatter the land seemed . . . and the fewer the homesteads.

Neighbors in Sweetgrass would be few and far between. I glanced at Rebecca and shook my head. Just over two months ago, when she revealed her intentions, Molly had protested and Mr. Gare did all in his power to talk her out of it. The Reverend Thomas had said it was too close to our father's and Ethan's deaths for her to marry; she should wait a full year, as was the custom. But all to no avail. Perhaps Rebecca had some of the Jessup stubbornness after all.

Now our house had been sold, Molly had found a position as a cook at one of the better boardinghouses in New Bedford, and we were a thousand miles or more from home, about to meet the man Rebecca planned to wed. As a concession to Molly and Mr. Gare, Rebecca had agreed to leave most of our possessions stored in New Bedford until she met Nate and decided whether they would be compatible. She would write as soon as the date was set and have the rest of her things sent.

But she did pack her wedding dress and a few other precious items. It was while packing that I noticed the likeness of Mama was missing. Thinking about the picture, I must have fallen asleep. The next thing I knew, Rebecca was shaking my shoulder. I opened my eyes to a gray day. Then I realized the train had stopped.

"You slept through the night." Rebecca sounded excited, though she looked more peaked than ever. "We're here. This is Omaha!"

I peered out the dusty train window, but all I could

make out was the station, a windmill—which I later learned they called a wind-engine—and other depot buildings. The brakeman helped us with our luggage and told us we could stow it in the baggage room until it was time to board our train for Lincoln. We had time to get breakfast and take our first look at a frontier town. The stationmaster directed us to a respectable eatery in a good hotel near the depot. He promised to send over one of the station boys to let us know when the train would be boarding.

We walked out onto the streets of Omaha and my heart sank. The gray sky had dissolved into a light drizzle. At least the rain would keep the dirt down, though we wouldn't be able to stroll much through the town. Not that I particularly wanted to. Compared to New Bedford, this place was a wilderness. The town looked like someone had glued a pile of packing crates together. The buildings, crudely constructed of wood, were mostly unpainted. There were no sidewalks to speak of, just raised boardwalks. The streets weren't paved, and the parade of horses, carriages, carts, and cattle being driven to the stockyards near the depot kicked up terrible clouds of dust. In the rain, the street would soon be a wallow of mud.

"Oh, I hope Lincoln is nicer than this!" Rebecca said wanly, grabbing my arm to pull me out of the way of an oncoming carriage.

I had my doubts but kept my mouth shut. Omaha was supposed to be the financial and cultural hub of the new state, while Lincoln was considered a wild western town. According to a flyer on the city we'd both read before we left, somewhere down these foggy streets railroad barons, merchants, and cattlemen had built exotic mansions overlooking the Missouri River. The place looked so dreary that I wondered if they really existed outside of the imaginations of the people who were urging settlers to move to the Nebraska frontier.

Rebecca looked about to collapse, so I directed her attention to the hotel across the way. "We can get breakfast there, like the stationmaster said," I told her.

Rebecca had had the foresight to wear her shawl and, sheltering our heads under it, we dashed across the busy street at risk of life and limb and plunged into the hotel. The lobby—more an oversized parlor—had a strange sort of grandeur with its crystal chandeliers, figured carpet, brass lamps, and red brocade sofas. The food tasted wonderful, especially after our days on the train with nothing but quick and greasy depot fare to tide us through. The food in the dining car had been too dear, and Rebecca was wary of dipping too deeply into our little nest egg. If things didn't work out with Nate, we would need some money to travel back home—or elsewhere—to start another new life.

We stayed in the lobby, reading magazines and newspapers, to keep out of the weather. A boy came by two hours later to tell us that our train to Lincoln was delayed. The earliest it would leave would be noon—in fact, it wasn't even in Omaha yet. We finally left Omaha at five that night, in driving rain.

The train crept toward Lincoln, stopping in the foggy twilight while a ghostly herd of bison made its way across the tracks. It seemed we'd only just gotten under way again when there was a brake problem, and we had to stop at a watering station. The rain was so terrible that we could barely glimpse the prairie out the window. When we arrived in Lincoln, it was almost ten P.M.

"What if he didn't wait?" Rebecca was near tears as we disembarked behind the small depot. She was fussing with her bonnet and her hair.

"Of course he'll wait. You're his bride. He's as eager to meet you as you are to meet him!" I tried to cheer her, though I felt pretty dismal myself.

The rain had let up, but the sky was dark and overcast. The kerosene lamps in the station cast small circles of dim light on the platform. Lincoln was as far as the train went, and everyone had to get off. The commotion was incredible, or at least seemed so in the half dark.

"Are you the Jessup sisters?" a heavily accented voice asked.

We both turned around. Instinctively, Rebecca took my arm. I could feel the fear running through her.

"Nathaniel Briscomb?" she asked, unable to keep the disappointment out of her voice.

For the man standing in front of us didn't look at all like the photograph she'd studied all these months. This man wore the strangest beard—blond, like his hair, but bushy and bristly and long enough to touch his chest. He looked about twenty-two—the age Nate Briscomb said he was. Tall, thin, and very big-boned, he had large hands and feet. The sleeves of his patched homespun shirt didn't meet his wrists, and the bottom of his suspendered pants ended above his ankles. He held a cap in his hands, and his eyes, colorless in the dim light, were wide like a child's. At first glance he looked simpleminded. It turned out he was just an honest, kindhearted person of simple speech and language.

"Nathaniel?" he repeated, and grinned shyly. "No. I'm Olaf. Olaf Swenson. Nate is my neighbor. When he found out I had to come to Lincoln for supplies, he asked me if I could fetch you home. That is, if you are the Jessup sisters." He paused.

Even in the shadows I could see the expressions racing across Rebecca's face. Amazement. Disappointment. Anger. Fear. I watched her swallow, then draw herself up to her full height. I must say I admired the dignity with which she asked, "Nathaniel sent you to pick us up?"

"Yah!"

I stared at Olaf, wanting to be angry at him. But I couldn't. I felt a little sorry for him. He seemed like a pleasant enough person. Nate was at fault here. How could he possibly not have come for Rebecca himself after writing her he would?

"And the train was so late!" said Olaf. "It is too late to go to Sweetgrass now, so I hope you do not mind, but I have done as I think Nate would wish. I have taken you a nice room at the hotel."

"Stay at a hotel?" Rebecca was indignant.

"Yes," Olaf replied quickly, and reached for my portmanteau. "It is a very nice establishment, run by a good clean German widow. It is a proper place for two young ladies. She is saving some hot stew for you and will make you comfortable after your journey."

Rebecca was shaking her head in disbelief and anger. She seemed unable to speak. "Mr. Olaf—"

"Oh, Miss. I am just Olaf . . . there is nothing fine about me."

I started to smile. "Or us, either. We appreciate your taking a room for us. We will of course pay you for that—"

"No!" He was vehement. "Nate would not like that. He is a good man who can provide for you himself."

"Fine," I said, picking up another, lighter bag. "We will stay the night. But how and when do we get to Sweetgrass?"

"We will leave at four. I must be at my farm by ten, I think. My provisions will not keep, and with the rain I am already late. Besides, Nate will be worried. There is no wire service from here to Sweetgrass. He will wonder what has happened to us."

Rebecca sighed and picked up her carpetbag. "Then thank you, Olaf, for helping us."

We let him lead the way down the dark, muddy street into a warm, welcoming building. The hotel was not as fancy as the one in Omaha, but it was clean, as Olaf promised. And after days on the train, hot baths were more than welcome.

Rebecca put off all my attempts to comfort her. "I am sure Nate has a good reason for this" was all she said before we crawled beneath the clean sheets on the bed. I myself thought no reason could be good enough to not come himself to meet his bride. Rebecca's heart might have been big enough to forgive him, but Nate Briscomb had already given me one good reason to dislike him.

Olaf was right about taking a room in Lincoln, even for a few hours. We were so exhausted that we slept soundly until his knock woke us before four A.M. Within the space of an hour, we had downed a substantial breakfast of corncakes, biscuits smothered in a rich brown gravy, ham, and eggs. Olaf hitched a team of oxen to the buckboard and hung a small lantern from beside the seat. When we set out, dawn was still another hour off. Above our heads and to the west was the blackest of skies, studded with stars, though behind us, to the east, I saw a thin gray line of dawn. At least the day promised to be fair.

The three of us crowded on the seat of the buckboard. After the train, the pace of the wagon seemed very slow. Though we bumped down the broad trail leading west from town, Rebecca kept dozing off. I pulled her close to me and let her head rest on my shoulder. Olaf and I didn't talk so that she could sleep, but I can't remember ever being so wide awake.

Stars blossomed overhead, and I longed to count every one of them. Never before had the night seemed so huge. But I was even more impatient to see the world around us. The grasses were fragrant, and the dark was full of sounds—breezes ruffled the grasses, night insects buzzed around the oxen's heads, animal noises rose up from the grass as we passed. Gradually, in the dim light cast by Olaf's lamp, I saw that the broad road narrowed to the merest ruts in the grass. Olaf urged his oxen in a more southwesterly direction and left what felt like road entirely. The rutted wagon path continued due west.

Dawn rolled across the prairie like a slow, peachy tidal wave from the east. All at once the whole world burst into song, and I felt as if my heart would break with joy. I had never heard so many birds, but they were invisible in the grasses. Just ahead, cutting across the pale landscape, I spied a hazy line of trees—we were practically level with the top of them. They grew up from the bottom of a deep draw. Olaf applied the brakes as we descended and crossed a shallow creek.

Rebecca was jolted awake. "Are we near yet?" she asked sleepily.

"Not quite, Miss Rebecca," Olaf said. "Another couple of hours. But the ride will be pretty now, and it looks to be a fine day, yah?" Then he slapped the reins, and the team pulled the wagon up the steep bank.

Rebecca snuggled deeper into her shawl and hooked her arm through mine. She rubbed the sleep out of her eyes and looked around. She was still as a stick, and her grip on my arm was tight. The wagon bounced up over the rise, leaving the river behind. The sun at that moment burst over our shoulders and lit the prairie with slanty golden light.

"Oh, Rebecca, it's like the sea!" I cried, and my heart soared.

"It is. It is like the sea. There is nothing anywhere but grass. There aren't even trees." Her voice was flat.

I did not want to hear about the bleakness. "But it isn't the ocean." For the first time in months I began to laugh. "It's land, and it won't swallow us up." I made Olaf stop the wagon, and I jumped down into the sea of grass. It came up past my waist and was damp with dew.

"You'll get your dress wet," Rebecca warned, but she began to smile a little. "You look like a little girl right now, Caitlin."

I tugged at my braids—I hadn't bothered putting

my hair up that morning. It had seemed pointless to dress up for the most rugged part of our journey.

"And your shoes will get soaked," Rebecca added.

"I don't care," I said. I pushed through the grass and found myself eye to eye with tall purple flowers. When I asked, Olaf said he thought they were called indigo.

"In some places in Nebraska, north of here," he said, slowing the team to my pace, "the grass is taller than this, taller than even a tall man's head. But," he added cryptically, "grass is grass here. It has the same stubborn roots, and tall or short it is difficult. No doubt about it."

But I didn't want to hear about what was hard that morning. I adored the prairie. I loved the grass. It seemed to have a life and strength of its own, and as I swam through it I imagined some of its spirit driving up through the earth into me. I began to sing and pick flowers. I gathered daisies and bluebells and armsful of coneflowers, and the purple things I could not name. Soon, though, I forced myself to climb back up into the wagon. I felt I could walk forever, but I didn't want to slow down Olaf's progress. The sun grew warm on my neck, and Rebecca put up her parasol to shade her face. After a while, I dozed off.

Suddenly the buckboard jerked to a stop. We were on top of a low hill, and the grass spread out all around us, swelling with the wind.

"That's it, Miss Rebecca," said Olaf. "That's your new home."

Rebecca barely let out a gasp. I gripped the seat with both hands and leaned forward. But for the life of me all I saw was a tall windmill, poking out of the grass.

"Where's the house?" Rebecca stood up in the buckboard and folded her parasol and leaned on it. She shaded her eyes with her hand.

Olaf chuckled. "Right in front of us. Blends in real nice, doesn't it?" He pointed, then shook the reins and urged the oxen down the hill. I don't know whether it was the scent of water or the sight of a familiar homestead, but the plodding team picked up speed.

I followed the direction of Olaf's pointing finger, and then I saw the house. It was no bigger than a fisherman's shack back home. Square and squat, it was built of chunks of prairie sod. Bluebells sprouted in great profusion from the roof.

"Whoa!" Olaf drew in the reins, and we pulled up into a small area of tamped-down dirt and flattened grass. Chickens squawked and scattered before the team, and two bedraggled-looking dogs came bounding through the grass toward us, barking and snarling.

"Yah, Pete. Yah, Blue. It's only Olaf." At the sound of his voice, their barks shifted to friendly yelps of greeting and their tails began to wag furiously.

Besides the house, several smaller sod sheds dotted the clearing. A sod-roofed dugout was carved into the side of a low hill. Above our heads, the windmill blades creaked; at its base were a well, pump, and watering trough. The oxen strained toward the trough.

Olaf saw me staring up at the windmill. "The first one in the valley," he told us. "Nate Briscomb is a far-thinking man. He learned about windmills and pumps when he worked for the railroad. He sees how useful they are. But he will tell you all about his windmill. He loves to tell his story." Olaf smiled at Rebecca. "You will marry a very good man. He has a big future here. Yah, he is a good man."

Olaf jumped out of the wagon. I jumped out next and let Blue, a black-and-white collie, sniff my skirt. Olaf held out his hand to Rebecca. As she stepped down, I could see her lip was trembling.

"Nate, I bring you your bride," Olaf shouted cheerfully above the crow of the rooster, setting the dogs to barking again.

Rebecca dropped Olaf's hand, fluffed out the skirt of her blue-sprigged dress, and patted her hair in place under her sunbonnet. She took a deep breath.

"Olaf?" a voice bellowed from one of the sheds. "Where have you been?" A second later a man appeared. His shoulders were broad and practically filled the narrow doorway, and he had to bend down to step outside. He was wiping his hands on a rag, and his brown denim jeans were covered with straw. He squinted into the light, and his frown shifted quickly to a wide grin. He tossed his sunstreaked hair out of his face and hitched up his suspenders.

In a few strides he crossed the barnyard. He looked from me to my sister and back again. His features were strong, with high cheekbones and a square, determined chin. He tossed his longish hair out of his face. He was tall and cleanshaven. His expression softened as he met my eyes. His were the most extradordinary blue-green I'd ever seen.

"Rebecca Jessup," he said to me, "I'm Nate Briscomb." He poked out a broad, calloused hand in my direction.

I was so shocked that I couldn't find my voice.

"Oooh, you are a fool, Briscomb. This is not Rebecca," laughed Olaf. "This is Caitlin."

Chapter 8

"**I**—I'm Rebecca." My sister stepped forward shyly and extended her gloved hand toward Nate Briscomb. "You said you got the miniature of my mother I sent you?"

I gasped. "You sent our miniature of Mama clear across the country?" I felt betrayed. Until Rebecca *married* that miniature belonged to both of us. What if it had been lost in the mails?

Rebecca cast a pleading glance at me. "I had no likeness of myself, and I couldn't very well have had one made without you and Molly knowing." She turned back to Nate, her mouth turned up in a shy smile. "Everyone says I look just like my mother— except for the eyes. Caitlin looks like our father, but has our mother's eyes."

Nate swallowed visibly and cast a sidelong glance at me. "That must be it. I did notice the eyes," he said, and then took Rebecca's hand between both of his. "But now I see my mistake." He bowed gallantly from the waist. When he straightened up he wore a mischievous expression. "I must have been blind. You don't look at all alike."

Olaf was grinning. "Blind—yah. Two lovely girls, but Rebecca's the one, with her hair yellow like the sun. Caitlan is like the night. And she is still just a girl, no?" He affectionately tugged one of my braids as he passed. One of the daisies I'd tucked in that morning tumbled out, brown and wilted.

Suddenly I felt foolish and very young. I wished that, like Rebecca, I had bothered to put up my hair and change my dress. My drab brown calico was travel stained and short, barely skimming the top of my boots. I probably did look like a schoolgirl. The thought had never bothered me before. "I'm near on seventeen," I called after Olaf, who was leading his oxen to the water trough. I only exaggerated by a few months.

Nate laughed and looked at me again, shaking his head. "Sorry for the mistake, Caitlin." Something in the way he said it made me look up sharply. He hoisted our heavy bags out of the buckboard as if they weighed nothing. Though he was lean, he seemed stronger than even the blacksmith Caleb Hawke.

"Caitlin's no little girl," Rebecca said, putting her hand on my waist and smiling at me. "She turned down a marriage proposal just before we decided to come to Nebraska."

Nate caught my eye again. "No. I'd not say she's a child."

My heart caught in my throat. Not even Henry Gare, when he had asked me to marry him, had looked at me the way Nate just did. I felt my face redden in confusion, but I was so red from the sun already, since I'd refused to wear a bonnet, that I don't think anyone noticed.

Suddenly I remembered I was angry at him. I stomped over to the buckboard and pulled down my own portmanteau before he could reach it. It was made of heavy sailcloth, with worn leather handles. It had belonged to my father once. Right then I didn't want Nate or anyone else to carry it.

"How come you didn't meet us at the depot? We were both disappointed about that," I said, meeting his eyes boldly. Then remembering Olaf, I added, "Not that it wasn't good to meet Olaf Swenson."

"Yah, I told Nate you girls might not understand. I said I would stay with the cow through the birthing." Olaf had finished watering his oxen and started unloading Nate's provisions—a bag of flour and a sack of sugar—from the wagon.

"Cow? Birthing?" Rebecca looked from Olaf to Nate.

"My cow, Daisy, is about to calf. She's ornery and wouldn't be comfortable but with me." Nate looked a little sheepish.

"You didn't come to meet me because of a cow?" Rebecca's voice was so faint that I don't think anyone but me heard her. And to tell the truth, I didn't know if Nate's admission made me feel better or worse about him.

"I was afraid to leave her," Nate explained further. He helped Olaf unload a few pieces of lumber and a small plowshare. "Now let's get you to the house so you can refresh yourself. That's a mighty nice dress you've got on, Rebecca, but you might want to change to something more practical. I've got to get back to Daisy.''

"Friend, shall I stay?" Olaf asked, laying a hand on Nate's shoulder. "I can be of help, maybe?" He gestured with his head toward the shed.

Nate clapped him on the back. "You've already done more than enough, picking up the girls in Lincoln. You have your provisions to get home, and no doubt your mother will worry about you not being back last night."

"Yah, my mama will worry, but my brother Bjorn is still home. Tomorrow he goes off with the trapper Jed Lynch to the Montana territory."

"And Jed's children?" Nate asked, leading the way to the house. "What is becoming of them?"

Rebecca and I trailed the two men, the dogs sniffing our skirts.

"The children will stay with us again." Olaf deposited our bags just outside the door of the house. He turned to us. "You see, we are not yet many people in this valley. And we live far from each other. I am an hour away. So we all must help each other. Jed's wife died a year ago. Now he has two children to take care of, and he hasn't ever broken his land. He is not a farmer in his heart. My mother helps when he must go to tend his traps up north and trade with the Sioux. So does my brother's wife, Kirstin. But Jed must marry again one day soon."

A loud moo came from the shed. "Daisy," said Nate, putting Rebecca's bag inside the door. "I'd better check her. Make yourselves at home." Then he hurried off. Olaf left, and Rebecca and I stood outside the door of the small house, surrounded by carpetbags and my portmanteau.

"Of all the nerve," I muttered as soon as Olaf left, "to stay here because of a cow when he had promised to meet you."

"I'm sure it couldn't be helped," said Rebecca, struggling to be loyal. We each grabbed a bag and entered the house. It had only two small windows, cut into the wall by the door. It was dark and had an earthy smell, but felt wonderfully cool. Rebecca took a few steps into the room, then stopped and looked around, dismayed.

"It's so small!" I gasped as my eyes adjusted to the low light, wondering exactly how three people would set up household in such a little room. It was for the most part a mess. Clothes were piled on one chair, and dirty pans and dishes were heaped in a washtub. There was a bedstead in the corner, and a plain but sturdy plank table with four wooden chairs. Cast-iron pans were stacked on wooden packing crates in another corner, and a large kettle dangled from a hook in the center of the hearth. A messy bunch of fresh daisies and bluebells jutted out of a broken crockery jug on the table. Nate must have picked them this morning. The sight touched me.

"Oh Caitlin!" A sob worked its way up Rebecca's throat. She clapped her hand over her mouth and took my hand. "Barns back home are finer than this. There's not even a stove!"

I watched her face crumble and, for the first time, the enormity of what she intended to do really struck me. Not only marry a man she'd never met—a man who had chosen to stay with a cow rather than meet his bride-to-be at the depot—but embark on a life that required a will of iron and a strength I wasn't at all sure Rebecca had.

But I knew I did. I had no idea that morning how long we'd stay here with Nate Briscomb, but until Rebecca came to her senses and decided to leave, someone had to take charge. I plunked down my bag in the middle of the floor and rolled up my sleeves. I pulled up a chair and tossed the clothes piled on top of it onto the bed. I'd deal with the laundry later.

"You sit down," I told Rebecca. "You're tired. Take off your bonnet, and I'll make tea. Then you can change into something comfortable, like Nate suggested. It's too hot here for corsets," I said plain out. To Molly and Rebecca's eternal dismay, I only corseted myself when I put on fancy dress, but Rebecca was always laced into a stiff corset with whalebone stays. I opened my bag and grabbed the first apron I saw, a plaid coverall made up from an old school dress. It was stiff from Molly's starch, and as I tied it in the back, I shuddered to think how awful it must look on top of my brown calico dress. But I couldn't worry about how I looked right now. I simply had to get to work.

"How will you make tea?" Rebecca had doffed her hat and was slowly taking the pins from her hair. I looked at the open hearth. The fire was dead.

"Rebecca Jessup," I scolded, forcing myself to sound cheerful. "You're older than me, and even I remember Molly cooking in the kitchen fireplace before we had our stove at home. We both know how to build fires, and we'll get the knack of cooking over one.'' I would have given my right arm just then to have convinced Molly to come with us, but since she was more than a thousand miles away in New Bedford, I'd have to fend for myself. I looked around for a wood-box and found none. "Except at home we had wood!" I grumbled. I told Rebecca to start changing her clothes while I sought out Nate.

The dogs greeted me, tails wagging. "Hello, Pete; howdy, Blue." I patted them and looked around, shading my eyes from the light. Though it was still morning and it had rained heavily the day before, the sun had already baked the barnyard dry. Beneath the windmill, meadowlarks squabbled and splashed in a small puddle. Just past the privy was a small, fenced-in pigpen. Olaf was right. Nate was a good provider. We would at least have ham for the winter . . . if we stayed that long.

Nate was in the shed, laying fresh straw in the cow's stall. Daisy regarded me with wide eyes and mooed. Nate looked up from his work. I noticed the shed was swept, and there was a clean animal smell about the place. Nate obviously took better care of his barn than his house.

"Where's your woodpile? I have to make tea. You've let the fire go out, and there'll be no noon meal for you if I don't have fuel." I sounded annoyed and a lot like Molly.

Nate's lips turned up in a bemused smile. "Wood is it you'll be having, Caitlin?" His voice was teasing. "Maybe you noticed on your way from Lincoln that the last excuse for a logging tree was about four miles back, at Sweetgrass Creek." He leaned on his pitchfork, and something in his expression challenged me.

I felt my color rise. "Nate Briscomb," I said, in a low, steady voice, "my sister is not feeling well. She has had a hard trip and is sore disappointed you did not come to meet us. I would think you wouldn't joke at a time like this. And by the way, you could have warned her you wouldn't even have a stove."

His expression darkened. "I could not come to the station and risk the life of this cow. We will need her, and I'd be hard pressed to replace her. As for fuel, we use dried-out buffalo chips, cow chips, and packets of dry grass. There's a basket full of them near the hearth." He waited a second, then added, "I suppose a city girl like you can't even start a fire." He propped his pitchfork against the wall and started for the door.

I blocked his way and glared into those eyes. Anger had turned them more green than blue. I would learn that his eyes changed with his mood. I pursed my lips and fought back the feeling of disgust—I had never heard of anyone cooking and heating with animal dung. But for the life of me I would not let him see that.

"I can build a fire, work a forge, and shoe a horse if need be," I told him. "I have, Nate Briscomb, even fashioned a harpoon sharp enough to kill a whale bigger than you could even dream of. So don't think you have the foggiest notion what I am capable of." Without waiting for his reaction I paraded back to the house, using all my will not to cry.

Within the hour, I had a built a fire big enough to

roast a hog. Beans were cooking, the tea was made, and I had already filled the largest kettle I could find with water from the well and hung it over the fire to heat water for washing up. I found brown soap and a stiff brush and began scrubbing down the table.

Rebecca had changed into her blue gingham dress and covered herself with a starched white apron. She had, thank goodness, come to her senses and packed away her corset. The tea revived her. In the larder she found potatoes, which she scrubbed and peeled. Between us we decided it was best to clean the house today and tackle laundry tomorrow, when we would have had a good night's sleep and could get started early.

"Speaking of sleeping"—Rebecca lowered her voice and glanced at the bed—"there's only this one room ..." She blushed furiously as her voice trailed off.

I didn't realize Nate had walked in and heard Rebecca's statement until he cleared his throat. At the sound I jumped and turned as red as Rebecca. He stood in the doorway, looking around. I could see the appreciation in his eyes. Even a couple of hours of cleaning had much improved the feeling of the little house. He wiped his hands on a towel. His hair was wet, and the yoke of his shirt was damp. He had washed up outside at the pump before coming in to eat.

"You girls sleep in here," he said. "I have a bedroll in the dugout. That's where I used to live until I built the house. I can stay there a spell until ..." His voice faltered.

Rebecca glanced down at her hands. "Until we get a chance to know each other—"

"And decide if it will be well to marry," Nate said plainly. He started to say something else, then looked at me and frowned.

Rebecca grabbed the blue-and-white tin coffee pot and fairly shoved it into my hands. "Caitlin, we need fresh water for coffee."

I rolled my eyes and marched out of the house. I knew she and Nate needed to be alone with each other. They had to do in a matter of days or weeks what couples back home did in a year's worth of courting. But I didn't like feeling as if I were an extra piece of furniture. I drew water at the well, taking my time about it. When I came back, Nate was at the table, straddling a chair. Rebecca had already dished up a bowl of beans.

"Nate's been telling me about the windmill," she said when I walked in. I searched her face for a clue of how she was feeling. Part of me wanted her to have already decided this life wouldn't work for her, and that Nate was too rough and tumble for her tastes. Part of me—already—didn't want to leave the prairie and move back to a town.

"I built the windmill because the creek out yonder is too far, and its water is not always deep enough to be good. Buffalo, deer, and cattle being driven to Omaha sometimes pass through and muddy it." For some reason Nate found it necessary to explain away the windmill. As the years passed, people came to think that he was some kind of hero. His windmill, like his barn, was the first in the county—or at least the valley, if you didn't count the bigger, taller wind-engines that hugged the wells near depots in railroad towns.

"Before the windmill, the well I dug was shallow. Midsummer, in a dry spell, I had to hike two miles to the creek for water. Practically had to squeeze the earth out for a bucketful at that," he told us now.

"And two miles back!" I marveled, giving thanks for the windmill.

"Two miles each way—for water?" Rebecca's question came out pale as winter sun.

Nate didn't seem to hear her. He finished his food quickly and went to tend chores before Daisy got further along. "Better keep coffee brewing," he said. "She might be at this for a while."

Which, as it turned out, was true. In the way of cows, she waited until after nine that night. Rebecca had just gotten into bed, and I was on my way to the privy in my nightgown when Nate came charging out of the cow shed.

"Rebecca!" he shouted, "I need help here. Daisy's having trouble. I need someone to hold her head."

"Rebecca's in bed," I said, stopping him at the door. I pulled my shawl around me. It didn't seem proper he should go in the house just then.

"Caitlin," he said impatiently, "get Rebecca. I need help—"

Before I could say more, Rebecca poked her head out of a window. "Is something wrong?" she said, stifling a yawn.

Nate explained the problem. Rebecca glanced helplessly at me. "But I don't know anything about cows." Then she grit her teeth and said, "I'll be right out."

We both went down to the shed with him. Daisy was standing restlessly in her stall. I went up to her and held out my hand. She backed away, but Nate soothed her. He looked over my shoulder at Rebecca. "The calf is backward inside her. I have to turn it around."

Rebecca froze in the doorway. "You want me to help?"

"No," I intervened quickly. I went over and took Rebecca by the shoulder. "No. Just make coffee. A fresh pot and bring it here in that yellow jug. Nate'll be needing it. I'll take care of things here," I said, though for the life of me I'd never played midwife to anyone, let alone a cow.

"Hasn't Rebecca ever been in a barn before?" Nate asked, staring after her.

I saw no point in lying. "Not to speak of. When we were young, Pa's brother lived on a farm in Vermont, and we stayed there awhile. Rebecca . . . well, we didn't need to do the outside work. She mostly sewed. To avoid sewing"—I smiled to myself at the memory—"I learned to milk and pitch hay."

So it turned out I spent a long night with Nate. Rebecca came with coffee. But at midnight, when the calf still wasn't born, Nate sent her off to bed. It was a long, difficult birth, and just before dawn the calf arrived. It was brown and white, like Daisy, with a soft, pink nose. It looked so helpless and frail, trembling on spindly legs as it sucked its mother's teat.

"Caitlin, isn't she a beauty!" Nate sat back on his

heels and beamed at the calf as if he were looking at his own firstborn.

"The luck of it—it's a heifer! We'll have plenty of milk and cheese to sell, even." His eyes glowed, and through the homespun of his shirt I felt his warmth and happiness.

Outside the night was old, and the morning hadn't even begun yet; but inside that shed I felt new and alive, as if I had just been born myself. Our eyes locked and we smiled like fools at each other, our fingers inches apart on the damp, soft down of the calf. The only sound in the barn was the quiet of our breathing and the rough scrape of Daisy's tongue as she licked her calf clean.

Then I thought, it shouldn't be me. It should be Rebecca sharing this.

Chapter 9

Sweetgrass
July 1, 1872

Dear Molly,

It is hard to believe we have been here in Nebraska only two weeks. I already love this place so much I feel as if I could live here forever. Stranger than that, Molly, I feel as if I have lived here forever—as though my roots go down deep in this earth like the flowers that are everywhere. They even grow out of the roof! When we arrived, the roof wore bluebells. Now it's covered with coneflowers, which are like purple daisies except the dark part pokes up and they are bigger. Nate says the Indians use coneflowers for some kind of medicine for colds and weak spirits in the winter. He says it works.

Remember how I always loved doing big, hard things? From the first day I came here, I have been called on to do things harder than I ever dreamed of. By the way, laundry is one of them—you can't imagine washday on a Nebraska farm. We have no stove and must boil water over an open fire in the kitchen, then cart it outside. There we fight off the flies and mosquitoes and bees and watch forever in the grass for snakes while scrubbing and rinsing. We spread our clothes out on the grass to dry. Nate says he will hang a clothesline soon.

The first day I was up all night with Nate because the cow had trouble calving. The next morning, when Nate was in the fields, a snake tumbled out of the sod ceiling of our house right onto the table. Rebecca actually fainted. I had to find a shovel and carry it outside. I bet it was a good four feet long. Nate told me I was very brave. He says I will make an excellent little sister.

Monday afternoon it was Rebecca who was the strong one. I think she has a way with people that I envy. Maybe because she is seldom angry and very gentle. Nate says she is gentle like a doe.

But I was telling you about Monday. Nate had gone to Olaf's—he is a Swedish neighbor, our only neighbor—to trade time. Olaf has had more trouble breaking the sod on his land. Rebecca and I were alone for the day—that happens often here. We were doing the wash in the yard when the dogs suddenly set to barking. We both looked up and saw—at first—nothing. And then a second later, someone was there. An Indian stood in the tall grass just outside the clearing that marks the boundary of our yard. Beside him was a small pony, unsaddled, as I guess is their custom here. The Indian stared right at us. His eyes were very dark, and I could not read their expression. I think we were both—fortunately—too terrified to scream. He walked slowly over to the water trough, took the dipper and drank some water, then brought his horse to the trough. I was still frightened, but less so. I suddenly understood that this man, like anyone, was hot and needed to drink.

Rebecca watched him drink and then, without a word to me, went into the house and came out with the small parcel of hard candy you gave us for our trip west. She walked, bold as could be, to the Indian. She handed him the candy. He took it, and then he nodded. And then, Molly McGuire, you will not believe this, he took off the beaded wristband he wore and gave it to her. Then he nodded, mounted his pony, and a second later was gone. He seemed to be swallowed up in the grass. Nate told us Indians would pass by often, and they were usually friendly. He said they were just people like us, some good, some bad.

I love this place, but Rebecca does not. A farmer's life, even back home, would be hard on her. Here it is more difficult than we could have imagined. The work never stops and is very strenuous. But as you will read in Rebecca's letter—coming with the same post—she has decided to go ahead and marry Nate. The date is set for the next time the preacher makes his circuit, which should be the first week in August. I think she is very happy, though I cannot *help wondering if this whole thing might not be a mistake.*

Not that Nate is the mistake. He is a good man and has the ingenuity of a real Yankee, though he is not a Yankee. He grew up in Ohio, before being orphaned and adopted into a family in Missouri. He will take care of her with all the strength in him. I think he is that kind of man. And I think you would like him a great deal. He has a strong spirit and a smart way about him. And he is not bad to look at, as Rebecca will have told you. Something in him will make a success of anything he does. But I do not think Rebecca has the strength for this life. I barely do.

Oh Molly, how I miss you! There is more to tell you. Before we left, you said I would have plenty of stories to tell just living here. I could go on for hours. But not now, for Olaf has come, and Nate and he must leave with our letters immediately if they are to return from Sweetgrass by tonight, and I so want my letter to reach you.

Your "lass,"
Caitlin

P.S. We almost named the calf after you! But since her mother is Daisy, we just called her Flower.

Before seven that morning, Nate and Olaf rode off in the buckboard with our letters, a message for the itinerant preacher, and the plowshare, which needed mending. By seven that night they had not returned.

After days of dry weather a storm was brewing; the evening sky had clouded over from blue to gray, and now had a green tinge to it. I smelled the rain somewhere in the distance. I had learned that the open space of the prairie made everything distant seem near, and what was near sometimes seemed far away.

I was doing the evening chores. After two weeks our life had settled into a routine. I did the heavier work and the outdoor jobs—filling the heavier cast-iron kettles, gathering fuel. Rebecca had taken over the cooking, the ironing, and the endless job of keeping the sod house clean.

"Was that thunder?" Rebecca came outside. Behind her the small window glowed with a friendly light. She had lit the lamp early so she could finish ironing. Blue tried to slip by her into the house. "No, Blue," she said absently, pushing him away. She squinted into the distance in the direction of Sweetgrass.

I hadn't heard thunder, though the wind was beginning to whistle softly through the grass. I watched Blue try again to squeeze into the house. I was puzzled; he usually hated being indoors. Pete kept sniffing the wind, his long tail drooping between his legs. Now and then his ears pressed back against his head. Like Rebecca he stared to the northeast, toward Sweetgrass.

"The dogs are acting strange," I said.

"The storm. They probably hear the thunder."

"Maybe they hear the wagon. Maybe Nate's back." I was surprised at how much I had missed him today.

Rebecca frowned. "They are late. Nate said they'd be back by five or so."

A small shiver of concern went through me. Since we'd been here there'd been no big storms, but Nate had said thunderstorms often spawned twisters in the prairie. He told us that if one came, we'd see a dark cloud in the distance spiraling toward us. We should gather the dogs and head for the " 'fraid cellar" right away. It was our root cellar, and where he stored ice in the winter. He had dug it deep and made the roof of polls and dirt and sod. He told us that the twisters here weren't as terrible as in Kansas, and he'd never seen one big enough to destroy the house, but we could get hurt by the wind or flying debris. I worried silently about Nate being caught on the open prairie.

Rebecca brought me the milk pail, and I went over to the patch of grass where Daisy and Flower were staked. I pulled up Flower's stake to keep her away from her mother and began to milk Daisy. Flower kicked her back legs up, and her eyes looked wild. I glanced back over my shoulder. Out of the corner of my eye, I thought I saw a shadow slide through the grass about thirty or forty feet away. I stood up quickly and peered into the graying gloom. I saw nothing. Daisy lowed nervously. Lightning streaked over the western horizon. Now I too heard thunder.

"Pete? Blue?" I called the dogs.

They didn't come. My heart stopped.

"Rebecca?" I yelled over the rising wind. "We'd best get the cows inside. They're testy, and I might need help."

Rebecca hurried outside. The wind was rising. The smell of rain was stronger, though overhead the sky still showed a patch of blue.

"Where are the dogs?" Rebecca asked.

"I don't know. I called. They didn't come." My

voice didn't want to work. My skin began to crawl. Again I glimpsed a low shadow, flickering through the cornfield on the far side of the house. I pulled up Daisy's stake and reached for Flower's lead. "Open the shed." I bent into the wind and tugged the cow and calf across the barnyard.

Rebecca struggled with the heavy door Nate had fashioned from old packing crates; I struggled with Flower. She was downright skittish now, bucking like an unbroken colt. Her terror was contagious. I began to shake, but I had no idea why.

"Caitlin, you're white as a ghost!" Rebecca cried over the wind. She got behind Daisy and slapped her backside to urge her inside. "Is there a tornado coming?" She held the door with one hand. Her hair had worked loose from her bun and whipped across her face. She twisted to see the sky.

"I don't know. I can't see. The animals sense something—something in the grass."

The words were barely out of my mouth when Rebecca's scream rent the barnyard. *"Caitlin— wolves. It's wolves!"* She stood paralyzed. Flower bolted straight toward the high grass and a circle of glowing yellow eyes.

Maybe it was Rebecca's shrill voice, or maybe the sight of two humans, but the wolves hesitated. It was enough. I slammed the shed door on Daisy and tackled the calf.

"Rebecca, get into the house; get the gun!" I yelled. I stuffed Flower into the dugout where Nate slept and kicked some crates across the entrance.

Rebecca still stood, her whole body shaking, in the middle of the yard. I grabbed her arm and shook her.

"Run. Run to the house. Get the gun, and stoke the fire," I ordered.

Rebecca stood a moment longer. "I—I . . . Caitlin . . ." She began to hang on my arm.

I pushed her toward the house. "Rebecca, we can't just let them eat the calf and attack Daisy. Do what I say, now!"

I had no plan, but I knew somehow we had to keep the wolves away. I raced toward the house and grabbed a stout stick. Leaving the door open, I hurried inside and lit the stick from the cook fire, then ran back out, slamming the door behind me. Through the window Rebecca handed me the shotgun.

The wolves had encroached on the barnyard. Pete jumped into the pigpen, and a great squealing went up. The noise distracted the wolf pack just long enough for me to dash back to the dugout. I figured Daisy was safe for the time being behind the stout door of the shed.

But Flower was vulnerable in the dugout. I kicked out the crates that I had jammed against the opening and set my torch to them. The dry timber went up in flames, and the wolves slunk back between the windmill and the house, whimpering and growling. The whole time their eyes were on me and on the open shed behind me. I backed up to the shed door, blocking their view of Flower and Flower's of them. I could hear her stamping inside, butting the narrow dugout wall. Then the rain began to fall. I prayed the storm wouldn't be a strong one or last long. A major cloudburst would put my fire out.

But the sky opened, and rain poured in sheets. The fire sputtered. The wolves weren't daunted by the rain. As the fire began to go out they neared the shed, slithering through the mud practically on their bellies.

"Go away," I yelled at them. "Go back." Then I closed my eyes, pointed the shotgun, and pulled the trigger. The blast shattered the twilight. The rebound against my shoulder sent me flying backward into the dugout.

"Rebecca!" Nate bellowed. Shots rang out. Rebecca screamed. I struggled to my feet, and from the opening of the dugout I watched as the buckboard barreled into the clearing. Nate was standing in the front seat, aiming his rifle across the yard above my head. Olaf yanked at the reins. Nate jumped off the wagon before it stopped. The team was frothing at the mouth and bucking. Nate shot again and again into the grass, and then the shooting stopped.

I stumbled out of the dugout, rubbing my arm. Nate saw me coming. "Caitlin?" He looked past my shoulder at the dugout.

"Flower's inside," I gasped, grabbing his arm. "They almost got her, but—but I shot like you taught me. I pulled the trigger."

"Where's Rebecca?" he asked, the rain streaming down his face and pouring in rivers off his shirt.

"The house. She's inside the house." I began to shiver. Thunder rumbled and lightning cracked overhead, but the storm was speeding off to the east.

Nate looked at Olaf. "Let's secure the livestock and find the dogs. I hope we haven't lost them." His words were efficient, but his voice was shaking. Pete was still in the pigpen; we found Blue in the house, cowering beneath the bed. The rain petered out as quickly as it had come.

That night Olaf stayed at our place. He and Nate

built a bonfire in the yard just in case the wolves came back. They would take turns fueling the fire and keeping guard. Rebecca was too frightened to go out alone to the privy. I didn't blame her. I walked her out. While I waited by the well, Nate came up to me.

"What you did tonight, Caitlin," he said, rolling up his sleeves and throwing some water on his face, "was amazing. You are truly strong." Just then Rebecca started back toward the house. "Thank you for saving the calf," he added, then hurried to Rebecca's side. He gathered her in his arms, and she sagged against him like a broken flower. He kissed her head gently and stroked her back. I couldn't see her face, but I could tell from the way her shoulders shook that she was crying.

"Poor Rebecca," I heard him murmur. "Everything is all right now. I'll keep you safe."

"Nate," she cried loud enough for me to hear, "I can't take this much longer. I can't. I can't."

"Ssshhh. It's all right now. Wolves seldom come here. It was just the calf that drew them. They'll move on from the territory soon. Meanwhile, Olaf and I will stay together here a few nights and keep watch." He tilted her face up toward his and kissed her lightly on the cheek. "I would not let a wolf hurt my poor little Rebecca." She shook her head dismally, and he led her back to the house, whispering words of comfort I couldn't hear.

And for the first time in my life, I wondered how it would feel to have someone take care of me like that. To envelop me in his arms. To keep *me* safe from something.

Chapter 10

All night long, wolves howled in the distance. As I lay in bed, wide awake next to Rebecca, the hairs on my arm stood up straight and my heart pounded like a drum. Outside, Olaf and Nate kept the bonfire going, and through a chink in the sod wall I watched flames flicker against the side of Daisy's shed. Olaf and Nate were talking softly.

I strained to hear the deep baritone of Nate's voice. The night of the wolves was when I learned what I needed to be kept safe from: not a wolf, not a twister, not a snake in the grass. I needed saving from my own heart. When I saw Nate kiss Rebecca, I knew I didn't want to be Nate Briscomb's brave little sister. I wanted to be his wife.

Rebecca had predicted love would hit me someday like lightning. Nine months ago in New Bedford I had scoffed at the thought. Tonight I was wishing I had only gone ahead and married Henry Gare. Then I would have never met Nate, or seen Nebraska. My eyes swelled with tears at the thought, and a sob caught in my throat.

"Caitlin?" Rebecca's voice was faint. "Are you asleep?" she whispered, touching my arm.

I closed my eyes and tried to swallow the lump in my throat. I was too restless to fake sleep. "No. Not yet," I mumbled, rolling over and burying my head in the pillow.

Beside me, Rebecca sat up and clasped her knees to her chest. After the rain the heat had come back, and we were sleeping in light nightgowns with only a sheet for cover. "Caitlin, I have never been so frightened in my life."

Me too! I wanted to tell her. But not of wolves. I was afraid of facing Nate in the morning. I was afraid the love might show on my face.

"When I saw the wolves their eyes looked so yellow." Rebecca let out a moan and buried her face in her hands. Then she wiped away her tears and went on. "I thought I might just die there. My heart pounded so! What if they come back, Caitlin, and you're not here and Nate's away? . . ."

I sat up and, out of habit, began to comfort her. "Becca, remember what Olaf said tonight. Wolves seldom bother people unless they are starving, and they aren't starving at this time of year. They're probably following the buffalo herd. No doubt they smelled Flower on the wind. Olaf says it's just a rumor that wolves prey on people . . . Yah?" I elbowed her in the ribs, trying to make her laugh.

"Not the wolves . . ." Rebecca threw her head back, and I saw tears streaking down her face. "Not just the wolves. It's everything." She turned around to face me and clutched at the sheet. Her eyes were a little wild in the dark. She rubbed her sleeve across her face. "Caitlin, I don't know if I can live here. I don't like this place. I'm not like you." She held her head between her hands and rocked back and forth on the bed. "I think if I were here alone, with Nate away so much in the fields and in town, I might go mad." She lowered her voice. "I shouldn't marry Nate."

My heart stopped. I knew I was supposed to say something like "You can't mean that" or "Don't be ridiculous." Instead I held my breath and hoped. For one wild, wonderful moment, I imagined Rebecca giving up and moving back to New Bedford, or even to a place like Lincoln or Omaha where she could become a schoolteacher while I . . . I could stay here with Nate on the farm.

"I can't live a life like this . . . but oh, Caitlin . . ." She threw her arms around my neck. "I really love him. I think I might love him even more than Ethan. I don't know how I can live without him."

Rebecca pulled away, then got out of bed. She wrapped her old paisley shawl around her shoulders, although the room was scarcely cold. She wandered over to the window and looked out at the night. The bonfire cast tall shadows across the yard. I realized then the men's voices had stopped. I heard the soft sound of Nate's fiddle, and Olaf began singing a sad Scandinavian tune.

I went to the window and stood by Rebecca. We watched in silence, then she said, "If I could only talk him into pulling up stakes and moving on."

"He'd never do that." Nate adored this place. He had put his sweat and blood into his land, and he would never leave it, not for Rebecca, not for anything.

"But how can I live with him here? . . ." She

sagged against me and draped her arm around my shoulder. "How, Caitlin?"

You can't. You mustn't. I thought, then felt, the hope drain out of me. "By letting yourself be strong," I told her. "You have your own strength, Rebecca. You're a Jessup, too."

She pulled away from me and laughed bitterly. "The Jessup blood is thin in me, I think." She frowned at me, and I thought for a second she could read my mind. "I am so jealous of you, Caitlin."

"Jealous of me!" I bit my lip so hard it bled.

"What I would give to be like you! Nate talks all the time about how brave you are, how strong."

Nate talked to her about me? About my strength? A hope brushed my mind. I remembered Nate's reaction that first day, when he thought I was Rebecca. Could he possibly care for me? Then I remembered how he had kissed her tonight, after the wolves were gone. My cheeks burned. What had I just been thinking?

Rebecca touched my face. "Caitlin, you're on fire! Are you ill?"

"No." I sidled away from her. "I'm just . . . burned by the sun."

"You shouldn't stay in the sun without your bonnet," she said, and made me face her. "It'll weather your skin and make it hard. Men don't like hard skin," she said with a soft, knowing giggle.

"It's late, Rebecca." I wanted to end this conversation.

"But I can't sleep," she said. "Let's go outside to where the fire is bright and be where the men are. I'm so afraid tonight."

She grabbed a blanket from the chest and my

shawl from a peg, and we stole out of the house. Olaf and Nate jumped up when they saw us.

"Don't stop," Rebecca said. She arranged the blanket across from Nate, next to the fire, and pulled me down beside her. She rested her head on my shoulder and smiled at Nate. "We're too riled up for sleep. Please, play that song again," she said.

"It's a sad tune," Nate replied, and our eyes met across the fire. We both looked away quickly, and my heart leapt up.

"Yah, a song about being far from what you love," Olaf said. "I sing it only when I miss my home country and the sea."

"I think Caitlin misses the sea sometimes," Rebecca said solemnly.

"But I haven't. Not since I came here." And that was true.

"I think Caitlin loves it here as much as you, Nate," said Olaf, regarding me with wide, honest eyes.

"Do you?" Nate asked, his voice muffled as he bent to throw cow chips into the fire.

"She was born to this sort of place," Rebecca added, and squeezed my arm. "We were talking about that just now, inside. Someday soon she'll find a life of her own here and make someone a wonderful bride."

"Yah, a good bride like you!" Olaf said with a chuckle, winking at me.

Nate picked up his fiddle and began to play Olaf's sad song. Olaf sang. Then Nate switched to some ballads he'd learned from railroad men and soulful Appalachian folksongs he heard as a boy. Olaf stopped singing and lay looking up at the stars. Soon

I could tell by the rise and fall of his chest in the firelight that he had fallen asleep.

Rebecca lay down, too, snuggled in her shawl with her head in my lap. I watched her watch Nate with love in her eyes, and I decided right then that very soon I would have to find someone to marry and leave this place. At last, serenaded by Nate's music, Rebecca fell asleep, still smiling.

Nate played on. I hadn't known he knew so many soft, sad tunes. I leaned back on my hands, careful not to wake Rebecca, and closed my eyes and listened. The music stopped, and I opened them. Nate was watching me from across the fire. This time when our eyes met, neither of us turned away.

We didn't say a word, or move, or even smile at each other. We talked only with our eyes. But I think that's when I knew. Nate Briscomb loved me, too.

The next day Nate yelled at me for the first time.

Olaf had decided he would stay at our farm a couple of days until we were sure the wolf pack had moved on. One man would stay around the house, mending tools and tack or hoeing our kitchen garden, a rifle close at hand; the other would take the second rifle to the fields. Although the corn would not be ready for harvest for a month or so yet, there was plenty of fieldwork to do.

All spring and early summer, Nate had been slowly trying to break the next twelve acres of ground so he could cultivate it next spring. The sod was tough and fought the plow. Even after the oxen had passed through a section twice, thick, twisted clods of rootbound earth remained. One person needed to guide the plow while the other hacked at the chunks of rooted earth with a pick to break them up.

I couldn't wield a pickax, but I could steer a team. So I was behind the plow, as Nate had taught me the week before. I was happy just to be near him. The storm the night before had cleared the air. It was a mild summer day, with an azure blue sky. I sang at my work, feeling sure and strong. Knowing Nate loved me was enough. I would never betray Rebecca. I had made up my mind that I would speak to Rebecca that evening. I would tell her I wanted to marry soon, too. I would move just far enough away so I wouldn't see Nate everyday.

Nate's team of oxen was gentle and obedient, unlike Olaf's. The work was hard for me, but it needed doing, and I felt a certain pride that I could work the earth as well as any man.

"Caitlin, what are you doing?" Nate's shout made me pull up the team. I turned around, and he was glaring at me. "Go home. Go back to the house."

"What did I do?" I swatted at the flies buzzing in a black cloud around my head. I had slathered on pennyroyal oil back at the house, but it wore off in time as I sweat.

"You're not letting the plow cut deep enough." He walked up and shoved back his hat. I peered at him from under my bonnet. His eyes had turned a cool green. "You're skimming the surface. No point doing a job halfway."

"I'll go back over it—"

"No. Go back to the house. Rebecca needs help. With the wedding just a month away, I'm sure there are plenty of things for you to do. This is rightly men's work."

I glared at him. "You're the one who taught me to do it. You're the one who said that out here, men and women have to share the work."

"My mistake." Then, without another word, he took up the plow and continued down the same row. I couldn't see any difference between his plowing and mine. I watched him go down the length of the field, then back again. As he approached I challenged him.

"I think you're just peeved at me."

"Why would that be?"

I walked alongside the plow and began breaking up clods of earth with my hand. "Because of last night." Then I remembered the looks we had exchanged across the fire. I felt myself go red. I shifted my gaze from his face and stared at a point over his shoulder. I said what first came to my head. "Because I managed to deal with the wolves before you got back."

Nate pulled up the team. "Did you, girl? What about the wolf on the roof of the dugout behind you?"

"On the roof?" My heart faltered. "I never saw a wolf on the roof." My retort sounded thin even to my own ears. I remembered now the way Nate had barreled into the barnyard and shot at something above my head.

"Right." He started up the team again.

"I thought you said I was brave."

"You were. But that doesn't have a thing to do with plowing—and Caitlin . . ." He took one hand off the plow and tugged his broad-brimmed hat lower over his face. "You'd best start learning more about woman's work. You'll be marrying soon enough, I reckon."

I glared at him furiously. "When and who I marry and what work I do is my business," I said, and stalked off through the broken earth, grumbling to myself the whole long walk back home. I felt like he had shooed me away as though I were one of the chickens. I wondered if the fire last night had bewitched me somehow and made me see only what I wanted to see, instead of seeing that, in truth, Nate Briscomb hated me.

That night—according to Nate—I milked the cow all wrong and neglected to fasten the leather loops that held the gate closed on Daisy's shed. The next morning, over breakfast, he announced that he and Olaf would take some time off from fieldwork to start adding a second room onto the house. "Needn't be too big. Caitlin will leave us to marry one of these days soon," he said offhandedly.

"Caitlin's room!" said Olaf. "For after the wedding. For a little while." He grinned at me, then poked Nate in a man-to-man sort of way. "After that, someday, it becomes a room for a child or two, yah?"

Rebecca blushed. My stomach knotted up, and I couldn't eat any more.

That day Nate didn't yell at me, but he didn't say much either. By the end of the week I realized we had practically stopped talking. By the day of the wedding, three weeks later, I was almost happy it was Rebecca and not me he was marrying.

Chapter 11

The day of Rebecca's wedding, our roof bloomed sunflowers. All around the fields were full of them, golden and grand, nodding in the slanty morning light. I was picking a bouquet for Rebecca in the back forty when the buggy pulled up. It was black and shiny, the kind fancy folk could rent from a stable in Lincoln. It was early for the preacher, and the guests weren't due for another hour yet. I had started toward the house when Nate emerged from the shed, leading Daisy and Flower to their pasture.

"Howdy!" I heard him greet the visitors.

A stout woman in pink gingham stood up in the buggy and folded her parasol. She looked right past Nate, toward me. I squinted into the sun. "It can't be!" I shouted. A second later I had broken into a full run, my basket of flowers banging against my legs. "Molly MacGregor! You've come for the wedding!"

Rebecca must have heard me. She stepped to the door, her hair tied up in rags to curl, her feet bare. "Molly?"

She reached Molly first and vanished in a huge hug. A moment later I buried my face in Molly's shoulder. I felt like I had reached safe harbor. "Molly, I can't believe it. You're here. You're here." I held on to her with a fierceness that startled me.

Molly soothed me. "There, there, lass. I've missed you, too." She hugged me hard, maybe sensing somehow that I needed her more this day than ever before.

"Is that? . . ." Rebecca's startled voice made me look up.

"Mr. Gare!" My mouth dropped open. He smiled and got down from the buggy.

He took my hand. "Caitlin, this place suits you," he said, but I noticed his brow furrow slightly when he gazed at Rebecca. She was rosier than she had been back home, but thinner than ever. She looked worn and tired.

"What are you doing here?" I finally worked up nerve to ask. It crossed my mind briefly he might have come west to try again to marry me.

"Molly MacGregor, what is that ring!" Rebecca was holding Molly's plump hand between her own.

Molly's color heightened. "Henry—Mr. Gare— and I . . ."

"Married?" Rebecca and I gasped in unison. I felt a great wave of relief and confusion.

Henry Gare took Molly's hand and put it through his arm. "I will tell you everything later, but when do we get introduced to the groom?"

Nate walked up to us, his hand extended. "Welcome," he said. Though Henry Gare was not a small man, Nate towered over him and seemed to fill the

91

space of the yard. "So you are the famous Molly MacGregor who taught Rebecca to bake so!" He sounded almost gallant. "And the same Mr. Gare who befriended Caitlin ..." He paused ever so slightly, and I think I might have hauled back and punched him right then if he mentioned anything about Mr. Gare asking me to marry him. "... Caitlin and Rebecca when they lost their father," he went on. "I reckon it's a fine thing for Rebecca to have such good friends at her wedding today."

Molly said something gracious, but I saw her study him. Then she looked from him to me, and her face creased with worry. "It's not good luck," she said suddenly, "for the groom and bride to see each other before the wedding."

"I'm not in my dress yet," Rebecca pointed out.

"And high time you should be. I'll help you. Come along, Caitlin. I'll tell you all about Henry while we pretty up Rebecca." Molly corralled us back toward the house like a mother hen, while Mr. Gare and Nate unhitched the buggy and tended to the horse.

While Molly helped Rebecca with her dress and hair, I changed into my Sunday best, a light-pink calico with touches of lace on the sleeve and pearly buttons down the front. I had shortened it in the fashion of prairie girls around these parts so it skimmed the top of my boots. The grass was too high for long skirts. Though there was no church in Sweetgrass to go to yet, Rebecca had insisted we wear our Sunday best each week to read the bible and have a prayer hour.

Molly explained that once Rebecca and I left New Bedford, she found herself missing us. Mr. Gare missed us, too. They would get together evenings in the parlor of the boardinghouse where she worked and talk. Soon their friendship deepened, and he asked her to marry him.

"But you're five years older than he is," Rebecca said, shocked at the notion.

"Why not?" Molly shrugged. "We both agreed we could live without having our own children, and when we settle in San Francisco—"

"San Francisco?"

"That's where we're headed now. On the Union Pacific out of Omaha. But when I got your letter announcing the wedding date, we timed our journey so we could make the wedding."

I couldn't believe it. Suddenly the wheels in my brain started turning. For one wild moment I imagined leaving with them after the wedding, putting another thousand miles or more between me and Nate.

"Why, Caitlin, you're crying!" Rebecca threw her arms around me and dropped her voice, "Did you care all along for Mr. Gare? . . ."

"*Mr. Gare?*" I repeated, and burst into hysterical laughter. "Oh, no, Rebecca. Not at all . . ." Remembering Molly, I grinned. "Though he is the kindest man I have ever met."

"Not as kind as Nate," said Rebecca loyally.

"Oh, I'd say kinder," I contradicted quickly. "He's been the best friend we've ever had, Rebecca Jessup, and don't you forget that."

Molly beamed, but she gave me a shrewd look. "Then why the tears?"

"I don't know—everything. Seeing you again. I am so glad you are happy. Now tell us"—I rattled on as fast as I could, trying to ward off any more questions—"exactly why are you moving to San Francisco. And what in the world happened to Mr. Gare's business?"

By the time the preacher came, we had learned that though Henry Gare Shipbuilders survived the financial crisis of the fleet's loss, Mr. Gare realized the heyday for shipbuilding in New Bedford was over. His brother had written from San Francisco about a shipping business there that could use men who knew about repairs and the building trade. With us gone, Molly no longer felt ties to New Bedford, and buying a property of their own in San Francisco to turn into a boardinghouse seemed a wonderful way to start a new life and a new marriage.

At Rebecca's wedding there were not many guests. Usually news of a frontier wedding brought families from days away, ready to break from the grueling routine of their work. But as Nate had predicted, an August wedding, at the height of harvesting, meant many people could not leave their stakes, even for a day. In our corner of Nebraska, most weddings took place in November, when people could break from work with less consequence. Still, there were a few wagons in our yard, and everyone who came brought food.

Rebecca's gown was glorious. She had, when planning to wed Ethan, sewn it evenings in New Bedford. It was made of silvery satin. Hand-worked lace trimmed the wrists and the high neck, and mother-of-pearl buttons ran up the close-fitting sleeves and went in a row down the back. I am sure it was years before our county ever saw a bride so beautiful or a gown so fine again.

Nate wore a new homespun shirt and vest Rebecca had made for him. Months in the sun had streaked his hair a golden blond. Everyone said they made a lovely couple. It was all I could do to look at them. But I had to endure their vows like bitter medicine. And like taking a tonic, it was soon over and done.

After the ceremony, people ate through the afternoon. Then the men played baseball, and I talked with Olaf's sister-in-law Kirstin about the idea of starting a woman's team like I'd read about in a Kansas City newspaper. When the sun set, we made a dance floor of our yard. We moved all our crates, the table, and chairs out of the house and arranged them in a big circle. Lanterns were lit and hung from the frame of the windmill and from poles staked near the house. They cast a semicircle of low light, and above us the moon was full. Half the dance floor was in light, half in shadow, but it was a pretty night and everyone was in the mood for music.

Olaf had brought his mother, Anna, as well as Kirstin. His brother Bjorn was still in the Montana Territory, hunting and trapping. A German family who had recently moved from Milwaukee to Sweetgrass had come, and though their three girls were younger than me, they flirted with all the men. Their father was a loud, friendly man who played an accordion. I counted five men for every woman— married, widowed, or any age, at that. The time wasn't ready yet, but within the year I felt I could find a man with a good claim—a man who would not be Nate but who would appeal to me more than steady, slow Olaf.

Nate fiddled some, and danced a lot, and I managed through it all to keep a smile on my face . . .

until Olaf bellowed that it was time for the traditional bride and groom dance. This was a custom I hadn't heard of back East. First the bride and groom dance together, then all the women guests pay to dance with the groom, pinning dollar bills on his shirt, while the men pay to dance with the bride, pinning money on her dress. That way a couple has a nest egg for their new life together. I imagined that being the bride's sister I could get out of it, but Kirstin took my hand and pulled me to the line of women waiting to dance with Nate. "Come, Caitlin," she said in her soft, accented voice. "You dance with your new brother now, as is custom. Yah?"

Molly bustled up behind me. "If his feet be as fast as his fiddling, I think I'm going to enjoy this dance."

Since there were so few women, my turn came too quickly. One minute it seemed Kirstin was polkaing across the clearing; the next, I had to step up with my dollar and pin it on his shirt.

"*Sister* Caitlin," he said with a formal little bow of the head.

I bit my lip and concentrated on pinning the dollar to him. I almost stabbed him. "You're out to wound your brother in the heart so soon," he joked, and people nearby guffawed.

I reddened. "Be still," I ordered, "or I'll really hurt you."

Then the music changed to a waltz, and I saw that Mr. Gare was dancing with Rebecca. I supposed the musicians thought he couldn't handle the spirited polka. Nate took my hand in his and put one hand on my waist. I rested my other hand on his shoulder, and we proceeded rather stiffly around the improvised dance floor. But as we moved, Nate's hand tightened on my waist, and my heart started racing. My hand was near his neck, and I felt his pulse quicken, too. I looked up at him to try to make conversation. But the way he was looking at me as he led me from the bright lights near the house to the moony shadows near the shed took my breath away.

"Caitlin" was all he said, very softly.

Before I could reply, I felt someone tap my shoulder.

"Time's up, lass!" It was Molly, with a bright silver dollar in her fist. She plunked it in the finely worked pocket of Nate's new vest. "My turn with this fine young man. Let's see what he's made of. It's said you can tell much about a man the way he dances." She smiled up at Nate, but as he spun her around in a slow turn she caught my eye. The warning look on her face said all. Molly knew my secret. The shame of it made me want to die. I was left in the shadows for only a minute. Then Mr. Gare joined me, and we passed the time talking about things back home.

I was to spend the night with the Swensons so that Rebecca and Nate could be alone. Olaf would drive me back the next morning. Mr. Gare and Molly would drive into Sweetgrass and stay at a small boardinghouse there. From Sweetgrass they'd go straight on to Lincoln and the connection to points west.

As the party broke up, Molly took me aside. "You'd best be wedding soon, Caitlin," she said, and touched my cheek with her hand. Her voice was stern, her touch soft. "There's no good of living here with them like this."

"Molly . . . I've not . . ."

"You've not done a thing. I know. *My* Caitlin is too honest. This is not your fault, nor Nate's, I wager. He is a rare man and has your strength, too. That's the sorrow of it. It's the kind of trouble that comes up when two single girls meet the same man. It's more than trouble—it's bad luck for everyone—when they're sisters."

Then Rebecca came up, glowing and holding her silvery satin dress above the dew. "Oh Molly," she said, throwing one arm around her and one arm around my waist. "You have made this the happiest day of my life."

I caught my breath, and then buried my tears in Rebecca's hair as the three of us came together for a long hug.

Chapter 12

After the wedding the months slipped by like beads on a string. One day it seemed the world was sunflowers and goldenrod; the next, I noticed the grasses were autumn bronze. Long days had turned short; balmy nights, frosty. Even when the sky was high and blue, there was a taste of snow in the wind.

It was the first of November, almost a year since we'd learned of the Arctic disaster. I was in the side garden pulling turnips. Nate had gone to Olaf's to borrow some nails. He would finish putting storage shelves in the root cellar the next day. Rebecca was canning the last of our carrot crop. I yanked each turnip out of the earth as if I were yanking my feelings out of my heart—or maybe, I mused as I sat back on my heels and wiped the dirt off my face with my apron, I'd be better off if I could just yank out my heart. The pain of Rebecca and Nate's wedding had subsided to a dull ache. And with it, I lost my will to wed anyone. I went through my chores like a windup doll. I was grateful for all the work, for it kept my hands busy and my body too tired most of the time for my mind to imagine what might have been.

The breeze stiffened—it was blowing from the north. I lifted my face to it, then sniffed. There was an unfamiliar scent in the air, slightly acrid but not unpleasant.

"Caitlin?"

I looked up. Rebecca had the dishpan on one hip. She was beginning to look plumper. Her blue wool dress strained across the waist. Marriage was agreeing with her. For the first time in my life, I was growing too thin.

"What's that smell?" she asked.

"I don't know." I stood up and wiped my hands on my skirt. I looked to the west. It was a growing habit. In autumn and winter the winds prevailed from the west-northwest. I shielded my eyes and squinted into the distance. Something was wrong with the far horizon. It seemed to be moving. Behind me the buckboard rattled into the yard. I didn't bother to look around; I could tell from the smile on Rebecca's face that it was Nate.

He walked up. "What are you looking at?" He followed my gaze.

"What is it?" I pointed west. "Why does the sky at the horizon look so strange? The sky is clear, but there's a cloud rising from the earth."

He pushed back his hat. "Looks like a herd on the move."

"Cattle," said Rebecca.

"Maybe." He shifted his eyes from the sky to

Rebecca. A silly smile tugged at his lips. Then, very gently, he patted her stomach.

"Rebecca Jess—Briscomb!" I cried, forgetting about the strange scent in the air and the cloud. "Are you expecting?"

"You don't know?" Nate looked at me, startled. "Don't you women share these things?" He frowned at Rebecca, coloring slightly beneath his tanned skin. "Got some stuff to put in the shed," he said, and hurried back to the wagon.

I stood there, wanting to hug her, yet feeling hurt. "You didn't tell me."

Rebecca touched my arm. Her touch was hesitant. "I—I wanted it to be just between me and Nate—only for a little."

Her blue eyes met mine, and for a moment I was sure she knew. "Caitlin, when you're married you'll understand. It—it's special," she whispered. "We all live so close here . . ."

I stopped her with a kiss on the cheek. "I understand." Then I planted my hands on my hips and gave her my best Molly look. "But you have to take care of yourself."

Rebecca closed her eyes and sighed. "I know. After Mama . . . Caitlin, I'm so scared."

"But you feel all right so far?" I asked quickly, looking at her more carefully. I didn't know a thing about bearing children, but to me she looked well.

"I've never felt better."

"Then that's all there is to it." I sounded definite, but a tiny fear pulled at my chest. "When . . . ?"

Rebecca turned scarlet. "May. Early May, I think. The wedding was August"—she counted the months on her fingers—"yes, May. That would be the earliest. Caitlin, I know we talked back before I married about you wanting to marry soon yourself. But do you think you can wait until I have the baby? I don't want to be alone here.''

"Marry?'' I hadn't forgotten about it. I just hadn't done a thing about looking for a man of my own. I hadn't the heart for it. The only single man I ever saw these days was Olaf. "I don't see anyone coming courting," I said.

"But there's that dance coming up when Olaf has his housewarming.''

I had almost forgotten it. "That's right. He joked with me and said dances are a good time for people courting." I pushed Rebecca's hair out of her face. The wind had blown up, and the smell on the breeze was stronger. "It's also a good place to meet some more women neighbors. You'll be needing them, too—we both will—when your time comes. Anna Swenson should be of help, and Kirstin. And I hear one of the new settlers up past Olaf's spread is a midwife.''

"Wouldn't that be wonderful!''

Pa had told me to take care of Rebecca. I had failed once, when news of his death came in. Here was my second chance. "Don't worry," I told her. "I will stay. Before spring I have no thoughts of moving even a mile away.''

"If it's a boy, Caitlin, I want to name him Jonathan, after Pa.''

We decided to write a letter to Molly together and went into the house arm in arm. It was the first time since the wedding I'd felt close to her.

"Rebecca, Caitlin!'' Nate's call had an urgent ring to it.

"What's wrong now?" Rebecca said, putting her hand over her heart.

Back in September we'd had a pretty hard time with grasshoppers. Between Nate's setting small brush fires, the right wind, and a little bit of luck, the swarm coming up from Kansas landed north of us. Now I didn't say anything. In a shot I was out the door. "Nate?"

He was standing on the platform at the base of the windmill, looking west. "Caitlin, come here." For the first time since the wedding, he grabbed me by the arm. His touch was like a branding iron, but I tried to ignore it. I had never seen him look so worried and afraid. He pulled me up beside him on the platform and made me face west. "What do you see?"

"Dust? Cattle, maybe." It looked a little worse than before.

"I've got a bad feeling about this."

Rebecca came up from behind us. She spied the animals first. "Nate, what are those deer doing in the cornfield?" The corn had been harvested ages ago but the stalks remained, stiff and pale in the November light. Mule deer, elk, and bison often grazed their way through the fields this time of year. But these deer weren't grazing. They were trotting through as if they had somewhere to go—in a hurry.

"I don't know. I've never seen anything like this," Nate said.

"They're all headed down toward Sweetwater Creek," I noticed.

"Toward water . . ." Nate frowned.

Then I saw the jackrabbits—three of them, bounding in the wake of the deer. The acrid smell that had been hanging on the wind all afternoon was stronger. "I think . . . somewhere . . ." I looked around. There seemed nothing to burn, but the smell was undeniable now. "I think there's a fire."

Nate froze to the spot. "Fire." He repeated the word, then looked at me. For the first time since I'd met him, he looked almost defeated. "The prairie is on fire. It's been so dry."

It was true. There hadn't been rain to speak of since August.

"Nate, we'll lose everything—the cows, the house, everything." I didn't add that we might even lose our lives. If the very grass burned, where would we turn for shelter? The idea kicked me into action. "We've got to do something. The Indians must know what to do about this."

"Sometimes they set the fires," Nate said, "to keep the grasses growing. But with all of us living here now, there's too much life and property to be lost." He jumped down from the platform. "Trenches. I started digging one last year at this time. Thank God there hasn't been a hard frost yet."

The trench ran along the whole back edge of the cleared land, bordering our cornfield. Nate jogged to the barn, returning with two shovels and a pick. "Dig around the house. Start now. We'll have to work together." He shouldered his pick and headed toward the north side of the house. "I think it's coming from the north-northwest. I can't believe I didn't realize sooner what was happening." Then he noticed Rebecca. She was standing by the well, looking puzzled.

"I don't understand, Nate. What can a fire burn here?"

"Everything," we answered at once.

She caught her breath. "What will happen to us?"

"Nothing," Nate said, sounding firm. "We will dig the trenches and douse everything around the house with water. And then when the fire comes, we'll set backfires to drive it off, and with every rag we have in this place we will beat it out."

Rebecca began to sway on her feet. "Rebecca!" I sprang toward her and caught her as she began to swoon. Nate helped lower her to the ground. "There's no time for this, Caitlin," he said in a low, desperate voice.

"Give her something to do," I whispered back as she began coming around. I raced to the house and came back with the smelling salts.

"In her condition—there's not much—"

I thought fast. "Yes, Nate. I know exactly what she can do. You start with the pick. I'll be over there soon." I waved the salts under Rebecca's nose. She sat up, and her face crumbled as she remembered the fire. "Rebecca, we need you," I said. "Just the two of us, Nate and I, can't do this." I made her face me. "Stop crying. Get up. Go to the house. Fill every bucket and pot and pan and basin with water. Wet down rags in the trough."

She stared at me blankly, then slowly stumbled to the house. I waited just long enough to see her come out. She looked dazed, but under both arms she held pitchers. "Remember," I shouted across the yard, "fill everything with water. Everything."

Nate was wielding his pick feverishly, putting every fiber of his strength into it. I went behind him, trying to shovel out the heavy earth. Fortunately the ground around the house was cleared, tamped down by the traffic of the buckboard, horses, and cows so that the sod hadn't rerooted itself.

"Nate," I gasped as I shoveled, "how fast will the fire come?" I kept peering back over my shoulder. Herd animals were still filing by. They were headed directly across the fields to the creek, two miles off.

"Depends on the wind."

Relief washed over me. "Good. The wind isn't strong."

"But it will be." He swung the pick with a fury, then looked back at me. "A fire makes its own wind, Caitlin. I've only been in a prairie fire once, out west of here when we built the railroad. It was a terrible thing."

My throat closed with fear. I felt for a moment like I too might crumble. Nate sensed my flagging spirits. He stopped picking and put his hand on my shoulder. "Caitlin. I need you. I can't do it without you. I can't beat this one alone."

We both looked back at the house. Rebecca was slowly filling buckets of water at the well. She returned to the house with them as if she were hypnotized. "Rebecca won't be of much help with this," he said, sounding tired.

"No. Not in her condition," I said sharply. "Of course not." Though we both knew what he really meant. Rebecca, pregnant or not, wouldn't be much use in saving Nate's farm.

By dusk we had picked and shoveled halfway around the yard. Then Nate opened the shed and shooed Daisy and Flower out.

"What are you doing?" Rebecca cried from the

well. She was tearing up old clothes for rags and soaking them in the trough.

"In a fire the animals don't stand a chance penned in. We've got to let them follow their instincts and run ahead of it."

"But Nate, we'll lose them," I said. "If not to fire, the wolves—"

"They'll be lost one way or another. But this way there's a chance we'll find them again." He let the pigs go and uncooped the chickens. Finally he drove off the oxen and two of our three horses. The most docile one, a pinto mare named Dixie, he led toward the house.

Rebecca watched him, wide-eyed. "Where are you bringing that horse?"

"Inside."

"Inside my house."

"Rebecca." Nate's voice was sharp. "How else will I round up the rest of the animals later if I don't keep her here?"

"I won't let you do that. It's uncivilized. People like us don't have horses in houses."

"People like us won't survive by being civilized." It was the first time I heard Nate angry with Rebecca. "Get out of my way, woman."

Rebecca's hand flew to her mouth, and she stepped aside. I wanted to rush to her comfort, but there wasn't time. There were still two sides of trench to shovel. Even so we would probably lose the dugout and the shed unless the fire moved more slowly than Nate figured.

By nightfall, we could see the glow in the distance. The whole sky to the west glowed a strange orange red. Above us the stars slowly faded as the wind blew the smoke in our direction. By eight we could hear the sound of it, like a steam engine coming from far, far away. Nate and I were still shoveling when, around eleven, I saw the first real flames.

I was so exhausted I could hardly speak. "Nate. It's here."

Less than a mile away, a wall of red was racing toward us. Some instinct made me want to bolt toward the creek like the deer and bison and rabbits. In the smoke, ghostly forms of cattle loped across our land, and then shadowy shaggy buffalo. With a roar, the fire jumped closer. The world turned to soot. Nate soaked his bandanna and wrapped it around his face. I wound a wet shawl around my mouth and throat. Rebecca huddled on the doorstep of the house, holding her belly, rocking back and forth. She seemed afraid to be inside the house with the horse.

We had doused the roofs of the house and out-buildings with water, and now we began to beat back the fire with wet rags. Nate leaped the trench to the north of us and torched the grass, setting a backfire. Soon we were surrounded by flames. I could see nothing, and I could barely breathe. Tiny fires sprang up everywhere. I was afraid the wooden blades on the windmill would catch and start to burn, but there was no help for that. They were too high for us to reach with our rags.

On the ground Nate and I tried to beat back the flames. A fire would start, and I'd slap it out. Nate would run across the yard and douse a tongue of fire with a bucket of water. But soon the buckets were empty, and the fire got ahead of us.

"Rebecca!" I heard him shouting above the roar. We couldn't see each other in the smoke and soot.

I remembered her in the door of the house. I stumbled across some empty buckets and nearly tripped over her, cowering still in the door and moaning softly to herself.

"Rebecca, get up now. We need you. You need to pump more water. You need to help fight this thing."

"I can't. I can't!" She grabbed my arm and tried to pull me down next to her. I pulled away. She grabbed onto my skirt. I ripped it out of her hand; the hem tore. "Rebecca," I shouted, "we will lose everything. Everything. Your wedding quilt. Pa's ship in a bottle. Mama's miniature. Everything you've ever treasured—even if we escape with our lives."

The wind gusted strong, and for a moment I glimpsed her face. She stood up, hanging on to the doorsill. "What should I do?"

"Pump water. Fill buckets. Use the rags. Keep the fire away from the house. That's your job. And watch your skirt. You don't want to get burned."

And then I raced to the trough for more rags, and beat and beat and beat at spreading fire until my body ached so much and my eyes stung so bad that I didn't even notice when the fire began to go out.

"Caitlin!" Someone called my name from a distance. I was still beating at the flaming grass, refusing to let the fire beat us. And then I stumbled in the smoke into a trench. Or was pulled there. I couldn't tell. I fell against Nate, and I coughed and cried until I got sick. He held me, and I clutched at his shirt. It was in tatters.

It was then I felt the pain in my hands. "I'm burned!" I screamed. I began to sob uncontrollably.

"Caitlin, your hands!" he cried as though he could

feel my pain. He took me by the wrists and pulled me out of the ditch. Somehow in the smoke and dark he knew his way to the 'fraid cellar, where he found the small hoard of ice left over from last winter. He slapped my hands onto the ice. I remember crying out, and then I must have passed out.

I woke up in his arms, in the dark. He was rocking me back and forth. He had tied rags around my hands and packed them with ice. "Caitlin." He rubbed his chin in my hair.

I could see again. There was still smoke, and flames flickered, but the fire was over. We were alive. I clung to him a moment longer, then pulled away.

"I'm all right." The pain seemed distant now. I looked down at my hands. The ice stung them. I tried to tear off the bandages.

Nate pressed my hands back into the ice. "Keep them in the ice awhile." Then, holding my hands to the ice, he held his hands on top of mine. "Caitlin, you are the strongest woman I have ever met. And the bravest . . ." His eyes devoured mine as the roar of the fire dwindled in the distance, like the whistle of a vanishing train. "You have helped me save this place. Without you—"

"We're safe, then?"

"I think so. The house is still there."

"The house—" I sat up and slid away from him. I pressed my back against the cold dirt wall of the 'fraid cellar. "Rebecca," I whispered, suddenly conscious of the warmth of Nate's bare skin where his shirt was torn. "Go now. Rebecca needs you." I was astonished by the power of my feeling. "Please . . ."

Nate said nothing. He touched my hair, and his

eyes were nearly as dark as my own in the flicker of firelight. He lingered one long moment, then he crawled up the cellar stairs, through the shadows, to comfort his wife. Distantly I could hear Rebecca crying.

I crouched on the cellar steps, rocking back and forth but dry eyed. My hands stopped hurting soon enough. I was not badly burned at all. I put them to my mouth to stifle my sobs, but they were wrapped in Nate's shirt, and they smelled like him. I couldn't stand it. I ripped off the bandages and grabbed more ice.

It was a long time before he came outside again. He led the horse to the shed. She was skittish, but she seemed to sense the worst was over. Nate went back into the house. I waited until the lamp went out, and the murmur of their voices died down. In the west I saw stars glow faintly in the sky. To the east and south, the fire glowed through the night. It was almost dawn when, like a wounded thing, I crept back into the house, to the small back room where I now slept.

Chapter 13

"**O**h, look at all the people!" Rebecca exclaimed as our buckboard approached the Swensons' stake. It was a Saturday afternoon in late November. So far the fall had been dry and clear. It was a perfect day for a party.

Half the county seemed to have turned out for Olaf's housewarming. It occurred to me as we rode up that since the wedding in August, we'd seen no one but the Swensons. Work for everyone had been too hard that summer and fall, with the grasshoppers and then the fire, for celebrating. And all our neighbors but the Swensons lived too far away for casual visiting. Nate's land was still the furthest settled place in that part of Nebraska.

"It's good to see all these women, no?" Rebecca's hand rested on her belly as she sighed contentedly and scanned the crowd for familiar faces. I knew she feared giving birth alone.

"They will be of help soon," said Nate, patting Rebecca's hand. She sat beside him on the front seat, a travel rug over her lap. I had stowed myself in the back, among the food baskets. In my lap I cradled Nate's fiddle.

"May's not that soon," she reminded him shyly, and turned around to smile at me as if I shared her feelings about needing neighbors. "But I long so for the company of other women—older women—to talk with. And here they are!"

She sounded so joyful I hurt. Until that moment, I hadn't let myself see how the loneliness of this place had eaten at her. The baby inside her was helping in some ways, but in others had begun to scare her. No frontier woman wanted to give birth without the help of other women nearby. And today we were hoping to meet the German woman who was a midwife.

Olaf's mother and sister-in-law were our nearest women neighbors, but we'd only seen them twice since we arrived in June. We had learned from Anna Swenson that when Rebecca's time was near, Olaf and Nate would ride out and find all the womenfolk they could and bring them to our house. We would host them until the baby came and for a week after. That was the local custom.

This party was Rebecca's first chance in a long time to see the women of Sweetgrass. But even for me, who had taken to the quiet of the prairie like a star to the sky, the sight of all those buckboards, buggies, and wagons, crowding the field across from the Swensons' front yard, was heartening.

As we pulled up, music spilled out of the open door of the house. I began to tap my foot, and suddenly I felt it was time to have fun. My deep grieving for my father, my pining after Nate—all of that was over and done. And though I was not as graceful as

Rebecca, I did love dancing. And dancing was a perfect way to find myself a husband. Someone to save me from myself, and from Nate Briscomb.

And to save Rebecca.

It was hard to believe she didn't see what was happening. I had distanced myself from her since the night of the fire. I, who had always shared everything with Rebecca, now told her nothing. I squirreled away my thoughts and feelings in the deepest part of my heart. I was scared that the most innocent conversation might give me away, for I yearned for Nate the way the grass yearned for water, or fire for air.

He pulled the buckboard up alongside a buggy. I hopped out and grabbed our food basket. I handed Nate's fiddle to Rebecca and left the chairs for Nate. While he tended to the horses, staking them in a patch of good fresh grass and watering them, we strolled over toward the house.

"Mrs. Swenson must be overjoyed." Rebecca straightened her shawl and took my arm. For a moment it felt almost as if we were just girls again, back in New Bedford.

"Welcome!" Anna Swenson came out the door of her new house. Her face was bright as a bride's beneath the thick gray and blond braid coiled neatly on top of her head. She wore a crisp new apron with her fancy embroidery work around the yoke.

She led us to the table, which had been taken out of the house along with the rest of the furniture. Boards straddled old kegs and packing crates. Every horizontal surface was filled with food.

"We put your food on the tables, yah? Then we see inside. I am so proud of what Olaf has done. It is a fine house. A *home,* not a dugout." She fairly spat the last word.

Children raced around the yard, playing hide-and-seek among the buggies. As we went back toward the house, Mrs. Swenson introduced us to women we hadn't met yet. I was struck at how many were new to the county. Most were married with children or were younger than me. Only one or two girls were my age.

The men began lighting lanterns, and some boys built a bonfire safely within the confines of a hastily dug trench. Out of the corner of my eye, I watched Nate. He moved easily among the men. He seemed to know everybody, and they all appeared glad to see him. He looked so tall and easy in his bones. He seemed bigger than anyone there, a solitary tree towering over the flat landscape.

I felt Rebecca's eyes on me, and I shifted my gaze away from Nate. I caught the eye of a man leaning against the side of the old dugout, talking to Olaf. He was of medium build and older than either Nate or Olaf, perhaps about thirty. He was dressed in the rough backwoods duds of a trapper—fringed buckskin shirt, furred hat. A shotgun was leaning on the dugout behind him, and a large hunting knife hung from his belt. As we walked by he met my eyes boldly and smiled a slow smile, then tipped his hat. His dark, longish hair was tied back from his face with a piece of rawhide, in the style of some Indians I'd seen riding by.

"Who's that?" Rebecca whispered with a frown. She tightened her grip on my arm and made me walk faster.

I shrugged. "A trapper, I'd guess, by his dress."

"I don't like him," Rebecca said firmly, glancing over her shoulder at him.

"We don't even know him," I said. The back of my neck prickled. I was sure he was still watching me as we approached the house. The idea half thrilled, half scared me.

Olaf's house was sod like ours, but bigger. Its new walls had not yet had time to sag. The roof was only dried grass now, though by spring it too would sprout its crop of flowers. Until now, the six Swensons—Olaf, his two brothers, his brother's wife, his mother, and aunt—had been crowded into a leaky dugout. Just last summer a deer had grazed on top of the roof and fallen through a soft spot. Anna Swenson had almost packed up the house the next morning to move the family back to Wisconsin.

Inside, the new sod house had been cleared for dancing. The dirt floor had been tamped down firm, then swept and sprinkled with water to lay the dust. It was nearly as smooth as a wooden floor back home. Chairs lined one of the walls nearest the door. Rebecca caught her breath at the sight of a cast-iron stove. I smothered a smile, knowing that Nate had ordered a stove from the catalog store in Sweetgrass; it would arrive by train just before Christmas.

After supper, Nate tuned his fiddle, Brian MacNamara pulled out his mouth harp, and another man strummed a banjo. Polish Joe, who'd come out from Milwaukee to seek his fortune, fingered cheerful scales on his accordion. And one of the Negro men from a family that moved up from Alabama after the war had made a kind of drum from one of Anna's washtubs. Nate struck a merry tune on his fiddle, and the other musicians followed his lead. A man I didn't know began calling square dance steps, and my blood started to course faster with the beat of the music.

Rebecca felt too poorly to dance, but she seemed happy to sit sipping lemon water and talking with a woman who lived just outside of Sweetgrass, an hour north of the Swensons. I was afraid at first that I wouldn't be asked to dance. I had forgotten how many frontier men were single or widowed.

I danced first with Olaf, then with his brother, then with a man named Matthew, who lived much closer to Lincoln and still worked winters for the railroad. I danced, it seemed, with almost everyone. I must have danced without stopping for more than an hour. Someone besides Nate began playing the fiddle; and, oh, I know it was terrible—but I wished he would dance just one dance with me. I wanted to feel, for just a moment, the way I did when I danced with him at his wedding.

But he ignored me, as was his habit since the fire, and brought Rebecca more lemon water. He stood behind her chair, his hand on her shoulder, avoiding my eyes. When the music started up again and Polish Joe led the group in a rousing polka, I didn't feel much like dancing.

I slipped through the crowd. The crisp night air cooled my cheeks. I made my way to the food table and poured myself some lemonade.

"Miss Caitlin Jessup?"

I looked up. It was the trapper.

"I'm Jed Lynch. I trap with Olaf's brother Bjorn." He spoke with a slurred voice, in an accent that to my Yankee ears was vaguely southern. "Olaf said you had come to these parts from Massachusetts with your sister."

I wasn't sure this was a proper introduction—or that I should be speaking alone to this man—but there was something about him that I found attractive. He was bearded and handsome in a rough, hard way. I sensed pride and strength, and he had my father's blue eyes. Besides, Olaf knew him.

"Yes, I'm Caitlin," I said after a second.

He drew some beer from a keg and slugged it down. He wiped his sleeve across his mouth and looked at me frankly over the rim of his crockery mug. He smiled at me, holding my glance. "Not often a new young woman—not spoken for yet—comes to these parts."

"I came because Rebecca was set to be married," I said, starting back toward the house. I paused long enough to let him follow me if he wanted to. I felt a little thrill of power. I had never before flirted with a man.

"You'll be married soon, too."

"Oh, and how do you know that?"

His smile broadened, but he shrugged. "Because too many of us are looking for a pretty gal to spend our lives with."

"Oh, so you're not married," I said lightly.

His smile vanished. "I was," he said.

Then I remembered Olaf had mentioned a widowed trapper whose two children the Swensons sometimes looked after. I put my hand on his arm. "Your wife is dead?" I said. "I'm sorry."

His face was stony. "That she is. Six foot under for a while now." He sounded curiously detached. "I got two kids. I'll be needing a mother for them—one of these days."

I was taken aback. We had known each other less

than ten minutes, and he was speaking of having intentions.

We were hovering near the doorway, and an Irish round was playing. I saw Jed's feet tapping. I was wondering if he might ask me to dance, when Nate poked his head out.

"Oh, there you are, Caitlin. I'm sorry, but I think we'd best be leaving. Rebecca's feeling a little faint and tired from the heat."

"Something's in the oven already?" Jed laughed.

I went scarlet. Men and women never mentioned such things as babies and pregnancy in mixed company.

Nate frowned but ignored the comment. "You'd best get your things. Is there a basket of ours on the table?"

"Aw, you can't leave yet, Caitlin. The night is still young." Jed smiled at me.

Nate stopped and looked at Jed. "Caitlin can't stay here. We live an hour away."

Rebecca had walked up behind me. She looked tired, but happy. "Oh, Caitlin, I'm sorry. I know you were dancing so . . ." Her voice trailed off as she spied Jed leaning against the sod wall and chewing on a piece of straw.

Nate looked from Jed to me. "Do you want to stay?"

"We can't leave Caitlin here," Rebecca insisted.

"We won't. I will drive you home and come back. By then it'll be midnight, but the evening's not that cold."

"Would you like that, Caitlin?" Rebecca asked. "Would you like Nate to come back for you?"

"It's too much trouble," I said, though my knees

turned to jelly at the thought of driving the whole way back from the Swensons' with Nate. Then I remembered my resolve. I had come here to find a man to court me to take me safely away from Nate. I looked up at Jed. He was smiling at me.

To Rebecca he said, "There hasn't been a dance around here for ages, and with winter setting in there won't be another until spring. And Caitlin is young. Let her have her fun."

So though Rebecca looked doubtful, it was arranged I would stay until later. By the time Nate came to fetch me, I'd be so tuckered out from dancing, and so full of thinking of Jed Lynch, that riding home with my brother-in-law would be safe as pie.

Chapter 14

"You're quite the dancer!" Jed told me two hours later. His accent had grown more slurred and southern with every beer. His skin glistened with sweat, and his blue eyes glowed as he looked at me.

The musicians were taking a break, and we had stumbled out of the house to get some air and catch our breath. I was heady from dancing. Jed reached into the pouch he wore at his belt. He rolled a cigarette, then flicked a match against his boot and lowered his head to light it. The match light flickered against his face and cast shadows on his skin. He took a drag on his cigarette and tipped his head back, eyes closed, savoring the smoke.

I struggled not to cough. I hated cigarette smoke. It turned my stomach, but I decided then and there I could learn to live with it. We were silent, listening to the music start up again inside. We stood very close against the house, and the rough grass of the sod walls scratched at my arms. I could feel the heat of his body through his clothes. It reminded me of being in the shed with Nate the night the calf was born—the feel of him next to me, the moment we shared over the newborn calf, the way our eyes had locked. Except Jed's eyes were not as kind. They were the blue of the distant sky in winter, and rather cold. I thought it might be because his wife had died.

Since Nate and Rebecca had left, Jed and I had danced every single dance. His energy matched mine. I found myself liking the strong grip of his hand on my waist, the way he led me around the room. He was a fine, hearty dancer, and I was aware that people were looking at us, smiling, the way they smiled at Nate and Rebecca at their wedding. In the corner I saw Olaf nod as he watched us, then speak to his mother. I began to feel like part of a couple.

I tried to picture myself kissing this man. I couldn't, quite, but I liked the feel of his arms around me, and I clung to him as we spun around the room. I thought maybe when I knew him better, I could get to like him. He had a strength that appealed to me. With him I wouldn't have to always be the strong one. Maybe I could wed him. Maybe I could have his children. The thought sent my stomach plunging and turned my cheeks pink.

As we danced, I imagined a wedding. I imagined packing up a wagon. I hadn't met his children, but children liked me and I liked them. I pictured going further west with him on a trapping expedition, far, far from Nebraska. Far from Rebecca and Nate. Now, standing near him in the dark, I began to hope that would happen. With this man, I might be able to forget Nate.

"It's a waltz." Jed's breath was hot in my ear. I realized his arm was around my shoulder. I remembered we barely knew each other. I could hear the shock in Molly MacGregor's voice now.

I pushed his hand away and said, "Do you want to go back in and dance?" I tried to sound prim, like Rebecca.

"Can't we dance here?"

He didn't wait for an answer. He tossed away his cigarette and pulled me closer to him. I tried to protest, but the music was lovely, and he led me in a slow waltz around the yard. The movement was hypnotic. We were still dancing when I realized the music had stopped. I stopped moving. He held me a moment longer.

"So, Caitlin, my love," he said. "You are looking tired. What if I drive you home?"

"But Nate is coming."

"If we leave now"—he paused and pulled a tarnished watch out of his pocket, snapped it open, and held it up to the light of a lantern—"we will be home before he leaves. It's eleven now. You'll save him the trip. He won't have to leave Rebecca in her . . . delicate state. Besides, I would like the time to talk to you."

"You have a buckboard?" I didn't relish riding home behind him on a horse.

"I will borrow Olaf's buggy and a horse. I'll hitch it up now. You tell Olaf."

I did. I was relieved when Olaf didn't object. "Jed will get you home safely and be back soon. If Nate misses you and comes here, I will tell him Jed is driving you home. But you should make it within the hour."

When we pulled out of the barnyard, the party was wearing down. Families were hitching up their wagons, bundling their children into blankets, and going home.

"So Caitlin, am I wrong, or do you fancy me?" Jed waited until we were halfway to Nate's before he said that. Until then he had talked about news of the coming railroad and how he hated the "iron horse." It had driven the game from the land and brought too many people. He liked the country wild and free, without all the rules and regulations people put on things when they start making towns out of perfectly good range land. He said he liked to live his life private, with no interference from anyone, to do as he pleased with it. I had hoped he would speak about his wife. He never did. He didn't talk about his children, either. "Or am I too rough on the edges for a city girl like you to take a hankering to?" he asked.

"I think that's a pretty question to a girl you've just met," I teased, glancing sidelong at his face.

In the moonlight I could just make out a little vein throbbing in his temple. He fingered his beard. "Oh, I think we're beyond just meeting," he said, then faced me and grinned. "We've been dancing all night. Out here on the frontier, why now, that counts for something."

"Oh, does it?" I said, half eager to hear what he had to say, half worried he was pressing me for some kind of decision too fast.

"Caitlin, I'm older than you." Then he winked at me. "But not too old for the likes of you, I reckon. But I've learned one thing. Time passes. Life is short. There's no time for awasting, at least when it comes to courting."

My heart was in my throat. "So Jed Lynch, then we are officially courting?"

"Officially?" He stopped the horse.

The horse snorted and looked around. He seemed uncomfortable in the moonlight, stopped in the middle of the prairie. I wondered if there were wolves around.

"Let's not stop here," I said, clutching my shawl tighter and looking out over the dark grass.

"Don't worry, girl. You're with me. I'm a mountain man. I can take care of you real good, need be."

He touched my chin and made me face him. "I need a wife."

I swallowed hard. "I—I know. Your children—"

He laughed. "Right. Well, I reckon they're part of it. So what do you say, Caitlin? What are you really thinking behind those big deep eyes?"

I looked demurely down at my hands. "Why Mr. Lynch, I don't know you well enough yet ... but I won't say I won't consider it."

He took me by the chin again and made me face him. "Oh, I don't think there's too much to consider. As for knowing me, I guess that can be taken care of real quick and sweet like ..."

His voice had gone all husky. Before I knew what was happening, he had pulled me in close. I tried to protest, but he stopped my cry with his mouth.

"Stop," I cried when I could speak. "This isn't right."

He pulled back slightly. His breathing was heavy, and he touched my lips with his fingers. For a rough man his touch was gentle.

"Shhhh! Don't tell me you've never been kissed—

a girl with your spirit." He laughed and pulled me back toward him.

"I never have!" I cried, insulted and a little scared. I hoped that would stop him.

He arched his eyebrow. "Ah—I'll teach you."

He kissed me very gently then. For a moment, as he kissed me, I thought of Nate, and I kissed him back. Suddenly my heart grew cold. I tried to pull back, but he held me tightly. His breathing got heavier and he began pulling at my shawl.

"Stop it, Jed. Stop it!" I pushed at his hands.

"Now, Caitlin, I thought you were enjoying this."

"No, Jed. This is wrong." I shoved him hard in the chest. He almost keeled over the side of the seat. My strength surprised him.

He glared at me. "I don't like teasing, Caitlin, and if you're scared of being in the family way, don't worry because I intend to marry you. I don't want another man to have the likes of you." He grabbed me by the arm and pulled me out of the buggy.

I pounded his chest, but he was too strong for me. A second later he had me in the grass. I hit and scratched at him and screamed to wake the dead, though we were miles from anywhere. My screams had turned to sobs as he tore at my dress.

"Shut up!" he yelled, and suddenly I saw the glint of his knife in the moonlight. "I mean to have you as my wife, one way or another."

A gunshot blasted over our heads. "What the blazes?" It was Nate Briscomb's voice. Nate had come to save me.

"Nate!" I screamed, and a lantern flickered over me, crouched in the grass. Jed looked up dazed, then stumbled to his feet.

"Your little sister-in-law is quite the tease," he said, wiping his sleeve across his face and staggering back toward the buggy.

I was crying so hard by then that I didn't quite see Nate's face. Not until he was by my side. "Caitlin?" His voice sounded like someone had ripped out his soul. "Are you all right?"

I couldn't answer. I curled up in myself and hid my face from him and sobbed. He stomped off after Jed, who was already in the buggy. He pulled Jed down and punched him.

I screamed again, remembering Jed's knife. In another moment, Jed might kill Nate—maybe me too—and leave us here. No one would find us for weeks. Or even worse, he'd kill Nate and take me off into the mountains with him. "Stop it, Nate!" I cried. "I'm all right." I said it over and over.

"Listen to the little lady. . . ."

I watched in horror as Nate yanked Jed to his feet. "No, you listen. You get out of this county. Now. Go back to Olaf's, get your kids, and leave. *Now*. Or I will have you run out of here—"

"Who'll believe you when I tell the truth about Caitlin?"

"I'll cut your tongue out if you spread lies." The steel in Nate's voice stopped Jed cold.

He glared at Ned one moment longer, out of pride, I guess, then shrugged and hopped back into the buggy.

"Remember, out of the county by morning. Men here won't tolerate their women being treated like this."

"Oh, is she *your* woman now?" Jed asked. Then he snapped the reins over the back of the horse and tore off into the dark. Later we found out he left the buggy not far from Olaf's and took off with the horse. It was two months before he sent for his children. He had moved to Oregon.

I think we both watched until the grassland had swallowed up the last glimmer of the buggy's lantern. Then Nate turned back to me.

"Oh, Caitlin. How did this happen?"

I was still crouched like an animal in the grass. I didn't want him to look at me. I turned my face away. I was so ashamed and embarrassed. I wished the grass would open up and I could vanish into it like a grave.

"Did he . . ."

"No, Nate, no . . ." I cried. "He tried, but you—"

"Thank God!" And it was a real prayer as it came from his lips. He knelt down beside me, but at a little distance. "Caitlin?" He reached out and touched my arm.

I shrank away. I never wanted a man to touch me again.

"Caitlin, what were you doing here with him? I told you I would get you."

"He—he asked. He wanted . . . to court me." I found it hard to catch my breath. I was holding on to the tall, dry grass as if it were a lifeline. I twisted it in my hands as I spoke. "I was thinking of marrying him—if he asked. Olaf seemed to know him."

Nate said darkly, "You can know a man's worth as a hunter or worker and not know who he is as a man."

"I shouldn't have come with him. I shouldn't have kissed him—"

"You did nothing wrong, Caitlin Jessup. Oh, you

poor girl . . ." This time when he touched my face, I didn't pull away. I put my hand on his to push him aside. Instead his fingers wrapped around mine.

His touch made me start to cry. The next thing I knew, he had drawn me against his chest and we were kneeling together in the grass. He soothed my back with his hand, making slow, gentle circles, and then he pushed back and looked at me. "Wedding a man like Jed won't change a thing." We both knew what he was talking about.

"No. It won't. But it would have taken me far from here—"

Nate shook his head. "I couldn't bear it." And then he touched my face with his hands, and I saw such love in his face. "Caitlin," he murmured into my hair. "Oh, I knew from the first morning it was all a terrible mistake. I had seen your eyes in the picture. I thought it was you. I saw you walking toward me from the wagon, like someone I had dreamed of my whole life. But it wasn't you, it was Rebecca who had come to be my wife." His sentences were all broken, and tears were running down his face.

I had never felt such pain from another human being. It went like a taproot down through my body into the earth. And then the terrible strength of that land seemed to fill me. I pushed him away, still kneeling, and cupped his face between my hands. "I know, Nate. But what could we do? I could never, ever hurt Rebecca."

Nate shook his head. "It would have been terrible for her to come all this way to marry me and then know I fell in love with her sister. I tried to ignore it. I tried to pretend." He looked at me helplessly.

"I do care for her. But ... it's not love." His words hung in the air between us. Behind him the horses stomped and shook their reins. Their breath was frosty in the cooling air. After a long silence he said, "But what will this do to her? What we've done ..."

"We've done nothing...."

"We've done enough," he said. And he was right.

He got up from his knees and turned his back to me. I struggled to my feet and straightened my clothes. I was sure I could hear my heart pounding.

He wrapped his arms around his chest and tilted his head back and stared up at the night. "I will not betray my wife."

My blood ran cold. "I would not have you—ever—do that."

"You must marry. You must leave the house. Soon." He turned on his heel and faced me again. Oceans of feeling coursed across his face. "Oh, Caitlin." He reached for my arm. I stepped back just out of reach. He dropped his hands to his side but continued to search my face. "How can I tell you to do that? To marry without love. To have some man ... what you have been through tonight with Jed—" he said, his voice starting to break.

"Don't worry, Nate. I can do what is right. I have my father's strength."

"It's your own strength, Caitlin. Be proud of it."

We rode back to the house. But with every turn of the wagon wheels, the life seemed to seep out of me as if I truly had been knifed.

‹‹∞››

Chapter 15

Before the week was out, Olaf Swenson came for dinner. In the way of men, Nate had somehow engineered the whole thing in the space of two or three days. How he got word to Olaf and what in the world he told him, I couldn't begin to imagine. But Olaf appeared at our door, wearing his gaily embroidered vest and his best shirt, carrying a pretty wreath of dried flowers and grasses that his mother had woven for me. He gave Rebecca some of Anna's rich pastry, made from the white flour and sugar and butter that she craved so these days. Also in his basket were a savory venison sausage and a loaf of good, dark bread to add to our table.

The men did most of the talking. Olaf boasted about how even with the grasshopper disaster and the fire, he had managed to have a good enough crop to get them through the winter.

After supper he asked if I felt like walking out for some air. "It is a mild evening, Caitlin, for near on December."

I tried to smile and followed Olaf into the yard.

Light spilled from the small window of our house. Olaf strolled over to his buckboard and leaned against it. He lit his pipe. I watched the tiny fire glow in the dark as he puffed at it.

"We are good friends, no, Caitlin?"

"Yes, Olaf. We are that."

"And I think maybe good friends might be able to make a life together."

I closed my eyes lightly and allowed myself one more second to dream. When I opened them, my vision of Nate cleared away like the dawn mist in the full sun of day. "They might."

"I do feel for you, Caitlin. You are the kind of girl a man can make a good life with here. Yah, you are that. Strong and sturdy, and with a fine heart."

I noticed he didn't look at me as he talked. "Olaf." I stepped closer to him. I took his arm. "I want you to know I have done nothing wrong—with Jed . . . with—"

"I know that, Caitlin." He patted my hand. Something about him reminded me of my father, though he was Nate's age. He was solid. Steady. But unlike a Jessup, he would not do something wild and bold with his life. He would make a good husband.

"Caitlin, life sometimes here on the prairie gets us mixed up. It is hard on a woman, especially. It is good for you to move from here—but to stay near to your sister."

"Yes." How much did Olaf know? What had Nate told him? What had he guessed?

"And I would like to say my apologies. Forgive my English; it gets difficult sometimes." He leaned on the wagon and dug at the dirt with the toe of his boot. "I thought Jed was a good person. He is not.

132

He is a very bad man. I am sorry I let you go off with him."

"Oh, Olaf! It's not your fault, all that. I should have known better. I should have waited for Nate."

"Maybe. Or stayed with us. I think that would have been best."

So he knew. Nate had told him something about our feelings.

"Will you have me? I am not much to look at. And I am not as smart as Nate."

"You are a fine man, and I would be pleased to— to have you," I said over the hoot of an owl somewhere in the grass. Then Olaf Swenson bent and kissed me. It was a kind, chaste sort of kiss. But it was not unpleasant. I would get used to him, with time. I was sure of it.

With Rebecca and Nate, we planned our wedding. Nate's smile rested on the surface of his face. Whatever feelings he had left in him, he had buried them deep, like me. It was best like that. The wedding would be next time the preacher came around. Only Rebecca seemed unhappy at the thought. She was frightened at the prospect of being alone with Nate when trouble next brewed on the farm.

"But Nate will take on a helper," Olaf told us as we celebrated our engagement that night over coffee and some of his mother's sweets. "We have talked of this already. Caitlin has been such a help here, but another man is needed to work such a large homestead. You can afford a hired hand now, with your crop so good, no, Nate?"

"I can, if you don't mind cooking for a hired hand, Becca. I will wait until after the wedding and see who's looking for work in town. The dugout should do nicely for a man to bunk down in.''

I sat at the table smiling and listening to the conversation. But I felt as if I were watching a play being enacted. I had arrived at Nate Briscomb's in June, feeling for the first time free to lead my own life. Now everything was being decided for me: who I would marry, and when; and what work I might do. For I sensed that though I'd still do farm chores at Olaf's, my work would be more in the house with Kirstin and Anna than with the men. I felt like I had broken some rule I didn't know about and was being punished for it.

As it turned out, I hadn't been punished enough. Not by a long shot. Just two weeks later, Olaf's brother rode in from checking his traps, took ill, and died of cholera within days. The Swensons' well ran dry, and Anna declared they were cursed in this place. She insisted they leave before the winter set in, even before they sold their claim.

Olaf traveled all the way to Lincoln and talked with the land agent there. He arranged that when his place was sold, the agent would send the money on to Oregon, where Olaf's family would be living in a small farming town. Olaf promised he'd send for me in the spring, when he was settled. He wanted see how the living would be before we wed. As Rebecca said, with Anna and Kirstin leaving, there'd be no woman for miles around if the baby came early. So it was good I would stay until at least May.

Olaf asked Nate to hire a hand now to keep me from the heavier outdoor work. A young Norwegian boy named Carl came to work for us that winter. His family had moved back east when the fire wiped them out, but Carl had grown fond of Nebraska. He was engaged to a young woman in Sweetgrass, Inge Larson. They hoped to save enough money to buy a small stake further west of us, where land was more difficult to work but cheaper. Carl would live in the dugout until summer, when he and Inge planned to wed.

It was a strange, peaceful time that winter. The weather was mild, with few storms. Carl took the buckboard to town once a week to see Inge and to bring back mail and supplies. Looking back now, I think I was like one of those flies caught in ancient amber that you can buy from a catalog. Time had stopped for me, and the fire in my heart for Nate seemed to die.

Olaf promised to write, and all winter long he did. The letters flew back and forth between us. His letters kindled no fire, but they did comfort me, and I began to look forward to each one. His written English was poor, and his spelling terrible, but he had a surprising knack of telling a story on paper. With each letter I got to know Olaf better. In his slow, quiet way he began to bare his heart, and I came to like him more and more.

And so the winter flew by. Rebecca grew big and lazy, and it was good I had become handy in the house. It was Easter Saturday, and Rebecca was sewing baby things from new flannel while I cut a dress out of some shiny pale-gray taffeta Molly had sent from San Francisco for my wedding dress. Rebecca placed her sewing into a basket and stood up with difficulty. She put her hands behind her waist and arched her back.

"You look uncomfortable," I remarked, scarcely glancing up.

"I feel uncomfortable. Imagine, another month of this."

Rebecca walked around the room to ease her legs, then sat down heavily again in the rocker Nate had fashioned for her out of willow wood he and Carl had found by the river. "I didn't think you'd come to love Olaf so," she said suddenly.

"I am not sure it's love I feel for him," I told her, and stared out the window at the sky. Though the sun was out, it looked pale and wan for April, and there was a dampness that even the fire in our new cast-iron stove couldn't quite chase away. I sighed. Moving to Oregon was at best just two months off. I ached to get on with my new life, though the thought of leaving my prairie home hurt my heart.

"You seem to wait for his letters," Rebecca teased. I returned her smile.

"True. He writes such wonderful ones. And with my coaching he is even learning how to spell!"

A strange look crossed Rebecca's face.

"What is it?" I asked her.

"Nothing," she insisted. "Nothing. Just a cramp, I think. I'm glad tomorrow's Easter Sunday. After our prayer service we'll have a true feast—and not more of these beans."

Though we had had plenty to eat for the winter, we were down to our simplest provisions. We hadn't had meat for weeks, except some bacon cooked in with our soups and beans. Mostly we ate lots of dried corn, cornbread, corn fritters, and johnny cakes.

"I think I'll lie down awhile," Rebecca said. She

got up and walked toward the bed. Halfway there she doubled over. "Caitlin," she gasped. "I think— I think it's the baby."

"It can't be." I shook my head hard. "It can't. It's a month early."

"Five weeks, five weeks early." She looked at me, her eyes terrified. "Get Nate. Send him or Carl for the midwife. The Anmudsens were getting ready for her last week; she must be there."

"The Anmudsens . . ." New settlers, their claim was forty miles north of us. "Lie down now. I'll get Nate. Maybe it's a false alarm."

"Yes. Maybe it is," Rebecca said, and the pinched look on her face passed. She began to relax. I threw a blanket over her, then forced myself to walk slowly out of the house. Once outside I raced to the back forty, where Nate and Carl were turning the soil for next month's planting.

"Nate—it's Rebecca. I think she's in labor."

Nate caught his breath. "It's too early, Caitlin."

"I know. Maybe it's a mistake. I don't know enough about it to tell."

"You want me to go for the midwife?" Carl volunteered, wiping his long blond hair out of his eyes.

Nate frowned and looked up at the sky. "Yes, Carl. You'd best go to Sweetgrass to find out—"

"She's at the Anmudsens'," I put in.

"That's north of here some forty miles!" Nate cried.

"Rebecca wasn't due for five more weeks. Mrs. Bremen said she'd be back long before then. But not this early."

"Then you'd best get going," Nate told Carl,

clapping him on the back. "But Carl, take warm clothes."

Carl scoffed at Nate. "It's not so cold. Winter's over. It's been warm all these months—"

"It's not warm now," Nate pointed out. He glanced uneasily at the sky. The pale sun was almost gone, and a bank of gray clouds was rolling down from up north. "A front's coming through. We might have a bit of weather."

Carl walked me back to the house while Nate unhitched the team and brought them back to the shed. A horse would have been faster, but Mrs. Bremen would need to ride in the buckboard. I took a deep breath before I went into the house. My heart was pounding.

Rebecca was pacing the room, her face pale. "I think my water broke," she said when I walked in. "I think this is for real."

"Then we get to see your baby sooner than later. We will have an Easter child. Surely that will be a fine thing." I steadied my voice and took Rebecca's arm. "Do you want to lay down?"

"No, I feel better walking. Let's go outside and walk some there. I need the air."

I held her steady, and we walked slowly back and forth from the house to the well. I tried to talk of easy pleasant things—where she would have her flowerbed come May, and what new vegetables she'd plant now that the seeds from her catalog order had come in. We even talked a little of Olaf and my own coming wedding. Now and then she'd get a strong cramp, but she seemed to bear it well. And for the rest of that evening, her pain didn't worsen. It came in waves, and Nate and I took turns staying by her, walking with her around the house and praying that Carl would find the Anmudsens' homestead soon.

But when I woke Easter Sunday, the world outside my window was white. From the other room, I heard Rebecca moaning. I jumped up, put on my dressing gown, and hurried to relieve Nate. "How is she?" I asked him, then looked at my sister's face. She lay on the double bed, her hands twisted around a pillow. Her color matched the white muslin sheets, and beads of sweat dotted her brow. Nate was kneeling behind her on the bed, smoothing her tangled hair and mopping her forehead with a damp towel.

"I'm all right, Caitlin," she managed to tell me through clenched teeth. "I can take it if it's not much worse than this. . . ." Then she clutched Nate's hand. "Is it soon?" she begged him to answer.

"Soon Rebecca. Soon." He glanced at me over her head, and I knew then something was terribly wrong.

"Will Carl be back in time?" Rebecca asked. She struggled to sit up. "I need to walk," she gasped. Nate supported her and helped her pace the floor. She collapsed somewhere between the bed and the chair.

"Soon," Nate lied, carrying her to the bed. "Carl will be here in time."

He told me to heat water. When I refilled the kettle, he put on his shoes and grabbed his coat to go outside to tend the cows and draw more water from the well. He opened the door and a blast of snowy air blew in.

Rebecca sat up. "Snow? Snow in April? On Easter?" And then I saw her face as she realized what had happened. "Carl won't make it back. He's caught in this storm."

Nate nodded helplessly from the door. "Likely so. I've never seen a storm like this, so late, anywhere."

And so that Easter Sunday wore slowly on. The snow fell so thickly that Nate had to string a rope from the front door to the windmill and pump, and then to the shed, so he wouldn't get lost in the white-out. By evening the drifts were so deep he could barely wade through.

The snow muffled sounds, except the howl of the wind and then Rebecca's screams. Nate and I did everything we could. And at midnight, after a day and a half of terrible labor, I was able to turn the baby around and, at last, he was born. Small and frail, he didn't want to cry at first, but Nate slapped him hard and he began to wail.

"It's a boy," Nate told Rebecca. His hands were shaking as he put the tiny infant on her chest. I will never forget her smile. She was barely able to lift up her finger to touch his small face.

"Caitlin," she whispered, and I had to lean close to her. Her face, her whole body, had no blood left in it. I could barely see her through my tears. "I'm going to Mama now. Though Pa, he isn't there with her . . ." She looked past me and smiled the sweetest smile. My spine tingled, and I turned quickly toward the door. But it was closed, and outside the wind still roared. Nate knelt by the bed, weeping into the sheets.

"Don't be afraid, Caitlin," Rebecca whispered, her voice fading with each word. "Take care of him. Remember his name . . . after Father . . ." Her voice trailed off, then with one last effort she smiled at me and then touched the tears streaming down Nate's face. "You two, you are free now. Please, please marry each other. Make everything right. Do it for me. . . ."

She never said anything else.

Chapter 16

The baby didn't give us time to think about what Rebecca said, or even to grieve. Not right away. We had to clean him, keep him warm, and figure out a way to feed him. Within minutes of Rebecca's death, I had washed the baby, and while I swaddled him Nate boiled some cow's milk. I watered the milk down and put some sugar in it. Then Nate tore up clean bits of muslin, which he dipped in the warm milk. After several tries, the baby began to suck. Finally, when he had fallen asleep, we both turned back to Rebecca. Without speaking, we combed out her golden hair, washed her, and made her beautiful in her wedding dress. Then Nate braved the storm and burned the sheets, so the blood wouldn't draw wolves.

The snow lasted two more days. Inside the house, we moved like puppets, not speaking, not crying, tending only to the baby, hardly caring for ourselves. I know now it was a kind of shock—we both perhaps had lost our minds a little. But I can't rightly say what I felt then, because I don't think I felt anything.

It was a week before Carl straggled back through the melting snow with Mrs. Bremen, who took over caring for the infant. And only then did I crawl off to my room and hide. Grief for my father had been nothing compared to this. This time there were no tears. My world dissolved in a kind of blackness.

For near on a month I drifted in and out of sleep and waking and fevered dreams. I learned later that Nate had asked Inge Larson, Carl's fiancée, to live with us and care for the house, the baby, and me after Mrs. Bremen left. Inge always seemed to be there, nursing me, bathing me, keeping me alive. She slept in Nate and Rebecca's bed, and Nate and Carl bunked down in the old dugout. I stayed in my room until the fever was gone.

When I recovered, Inge helped me bathe and dress and was at my side as I stood in the doorway of the house. The prairie spring hit me full force. The late May sun blazed like fire, and the whole world was in bloom. I was weak from weeks of shock and fever, and in spite of the sun I felt cold beneath the old paisley shawl that Inge had wrapped around my shoulders. I could smell the scent of Rebecca's lavender soap on the shawl. I hugged it closer around me as we stood a moment at the door.

"Let your eyes get used to the light, Miss Caitlin," Inge said. "You've been in the dark so long and you're weak as a kitten, but soon you'll be fine as can be. Yah, I believe that. You are a strong woman."

I closed my eyes against the light. *A strong woman.* The day Rebecca died, I think I was still a girl. As for strength, I had grown so thin that my blue calico hung on me like a bedsheet, and I barely had the strength to walk. I held onto Inge and, keeping my eyes closed, let her lead me across the yard.

Looking back now, I realize God had been kind to me after all. That first day outside, I felt as new as Rebecca's baby. As I breathed in the scent of wild strawberries, the air seemed so sweet that I began to cry softly.

"Do you want to go back in?"

"No, Inge," I said, and my voice sounded as rusty as an old hinge from lack of use. "No, I want to stay out. Today—today ... I need to be up and out ..." This was the day the preacher was coming to Sweetgrass. He would come to the farm to baptize the baby and to say a prayer for Rebecca.

"Let's go to the well," said Inge. "I will wash your hair, and it will dry in the sun. Soon it will shine again."

She guided me across the yard. First Blue, then Pete, came running up to me. I forced my eyes open, and though they watered from the brightness, I looked down at the dogs and patted them, fancying that they were smiling at me. Touching Blue's silky coat seemed to give me strength. I sat on the edge of the water trough and looked up at Inge. Her blue eyes reminded me of Rebecca's, though her hair was the color of ripe wheat and plaited into one heavy braid down her back. Unlike Rebecca, Inge had strong features and rosy cheeks. She began taking the combs and pins out of my hair.

I looked down at my hands. They lay limp and palms up in my lap. They seemed to belong to someone else. As I stared at them, a shadow fell across me.

"Caitlin?"

It was Nate. I looked up at him, and the feeling of being newborn vanished. Nate's face was drawn, and he had grown thinner. His expression was serious, but his eyes were full of . . . I couldn't tell what exactly. Joy, relief, sorrow, pain. Maybe all of those.

"Nate?" I said when at last I found my voice. Inge started away, but I grabbed her skirt. I hadn't spoken to Nate since Rebecca's death, or barely, just to care for the baby before Mrs. Bremen came. Since then—incredible as it seemed—I had forgotten all about him. But with him standing there, towering above me, looking so strong and real, everything rushed back to me in a torrent. Rebecca's words on her deathbed rang in my ear—*marry each other*. Somehow she had known all along. The world began to spin slightly, but I gripped the edge of the trough and forced my heart to slow down. Gradually the faintness passed.

"Are you better now?" Nate asked.

"I think so," I said, looking down at the ground. "Inge has been so good to me."

"She saved your life." He put it simply, but his voice shook, and it wasn't until much later that I learned Nate had almost lost all of us—Rebecca, the baby, and even me. Now he paused, I think waiting for me to say something else. But I couldn't face him.

"Caitlin is tired, Nate," Inge broke in. "I must help her wash her hair, yah? Then she should rest some before the preacher comes later."

Nate nodded. He hesitated, then crouched down in front of me. I still didn't meet his eyes. "This came for you," he said, and put an unopened envelope in my lap. "It's from Olaf. I had written him about

145

Rebecca and little Jonathan.'' I realized he was care-ful not to touch me.

''I'll read it later,'' I made myself promise.

That afternoon, when the shadows were long, the preacher came, and for the first time since we had buried Rebecca the week after the storm, I saw her grave. It was behind the house, and wildflowers and tall grasses pressed against the small fence Nate had built around the grave site. He had carved a cross, and already grass and bluebells were sprouting over the freshly dug earth.

People came from all around to be with us at the service. Nate had letters from Olaf and Molly, and he read the words they sent about Rebecca. Nate's voice, and the preacher's prayers, and the gurgling of the little baby in the background all served to soothe my soul a little. Everyone placed a flower on the grave, then quietly filed to the front yard of the house. Neighbors had brought food and laid it out, and among all our friends and neighbors, a strange peace slowly filled my heart. Rebecca seemed to have somehow been there with us, and she had no bitterness or anger or sorrow. I think that evening I began to heal.

It was a late August night and the moon was full. Nate, Carl, and some other men were still in the fields trying to get in the last of the harvest before the frost. Inge had ridden to the fields on one of the horses, taking a jug of hot coffee and some sweet rolls out to the men. I knew she wanted to be with her Carl. They were getting married the following week, when the preacher came through back through

Sweetgrass after his journey to the new settlements west of us.

I had stayed behind in the house with Jonathan. He lay asleep in the cradle Nate had carved for him. I was at the foot of the double bed in the main room, sorting through the old sea chest Rebecca and I had brought from New Bedford only a little more than a year ago. I had thought to give Inge some of Rebecca's things to start her household with—the carefully embroidered sheets and towels and some of the good cast-iron cook pots we had never even used, since Nate already had his own. The hard-packed floor of the sod house was littered with piles of Rebecca's mementos: programs from dances, from concerts at the Liberty Theatre, from lectures she had gone to with Ethan back at the Lyceum. There were flowers pressed from bouquets, and faded ribbons, and Pa's ship in a bottle.

A cool breeze blew through the open door of the house and rustled a small, neatly folded square of tissue paper on top of one of Rebecca's gowns. I unwrapped it carefully and felt my heart leap to my throat. It was Mama's miniature. My hand trembled as I picked it up and held it to the flickering candlelight. Rebecca seemed to look back at me from the oval frame. I sat back on my heels, staring at it until the image itself blurred. As I looked at the miniature, I fancied it might speak to me—might tell me what to do next.

Though Carl and Inge would stay at the house awhile after marrying, Carl had already bought out someone's claim to a small plot of bottomland near Sweetwater Creek. As soon as he built a house, they'd move out of Nate's place. I couldn't stay on alone with Nate, and I didn't know where to go, what to do. I pressed the miniature to my cheek and prayed for some sort of answer. "How can I marry him," I whispered to the empty room. We hadn't even really spoken since the few words we'd exchanged before Rebecca's funeral, when he handed me Olaf's letter.

Dear Olaf—I couldn't even go to him now. His letter had made that clear. In it Olaf had broken off our engagement. He told me that now that Rebecca had gone to be with the angels, I should marry Nate, because that was what was always meant to be, ever since Nate had taken me for Rebecca that first day we met. I wondered what Olaf would say now, given the silence that had grown up between Nate and me. I thought that whatever had been meant to be between me and Nate had died with Rebecca.

"You found your mama's likeness." Nate's voice made me jump.

I felt my cheeks color, as if I had been caught doing something wrong. "Yes." I made myself look up at him. He was standing in the door, leaning on a scythe. I scrambled to my feet and started to tuck the miniature in my pocket.

"Don't." The pain in his voice stopped me. He leaned the scythe against the door and walked into the room. He held out his hand. "I haven't looked at this since the day I dug that grave for Rebecca," he said.

I dropped the miniature into his palm. His big hand seemed to swallow it up. He closed his fist around it without looking at the likeness. The grief on his face broke my heart. *Nate had really loved Rebecca.* I knew that now. And the thought hurt more than anything I could imagine. But at the same time, I felt relieved. Rebecca had, at least for a while, known love.

"Would you like coffee?" I said, needing to turn my back to him. As I stirred the coals in the stove, I thought my heart would burst.

"No, Caitlin. We must talk."

I looked back over my shoulder. Nate's eyes were glistening. He motioned toward the door. "It's a nice evening outside, but cool." He took my shawl from a hook by the door and handed it to me.

Heart pounding, I followed him out. *Nate is going to send me away,* I thought, feeling that part of me would die when I left this place. The dew was damp on my feet, and the tall grass made a swishing sound as I walked. The air was full of the sound of crickets, and in the moonlight the goldenrod glowed a ghostly white. Pale clouds scudded across the moon, and off to the west in the back forty I glimpsed the glow of lanterns as Carl and some neighbors guided teams through the fields.

Nate stopped beneath the windmill. I stopped a little behind him. Above us the wooden blades spun briskly. He gazed out across the night. Then, without looking at me, he reached down and took my hand. It was the first time we had touched since that terrible time after Nate ordered Jed Lynch from the county.

His touch sent a chill up my spine. "I can't, Nate," I whispered, trying to pull my hand away. "I know . . . you—you love her still, Nate."

Nate's grip tightened. "I will always love her . . ." Half his face was in shadow, half lit up by the moon. "But Caitlin . . . she was the one who should have been my sister. It has been—always—you." The words came with such difficulty, and suddenly I was overwhelmed with grief. Not for Rebecca, but for Nate. All these months alone, without Rebecca, and me wrapped in my own confused, grief-stricken silence.

"Nate . . ." was all I could say.

"I love you, Caitlin, I always have." He put his hand under my chin and turned my face toward his. I could feel the blood coursing through his veins and somehow giving me new life. Still, his hand was trembling.

I pulled back. I couldn't help it. All the passion I had ever felt for Nate was still there—I felt it surging through me right below the surface. But I felt ashamed. "I feel as if she's watching, as if she's everywhere. . . ."

"Maybe she is." His voice was awed. He stepped away and said, "You know what I think, Caitlin?" He hunkered down in the tall dark grass and stared out at the bracelet of stars hanging faint in the moonlight over the western horizon. "I think when a person dies, their love spills out everywhere. Rebecca loved us very much. Her love is like your ocean, Caitlin, washing over all of us. You, me, Jonathan."

Then he turned to me, his face pale in the moonlight. "Will you marry me, Caitlin, when the preacher comes next week to marry Carl and Inge? I know it is soon. Too soon. But we can't wait—and Rebecca wouldn't want us to. And Jonathan already thinks you are his mother."

I put my hands over my face to shut out Nate and the world. What I answered would change the rest of my life. Finally I dropped my hands to my side and looked up at Nate. His eyes shone dark in the moonlight. "Yes, Nate. I will marry you."

He gathered me into his arms, and the windmill whirled above us, making a strange music. Through the thin cotton fabric of his workshirt, I could feel his heart pounding against my chest and every fiber of my being felt like singing. He lowered his face over mine, but before our lips met I reached up and touched his face. I traced his features, one by one—his dear lips, his strong chin, the lids of his eyes, and his long lashes. I felt like a blind person, learning by touch first, then finally seeing for the first time.

Except through my tears by then I couldn't see anything.

Chapter 17

It was early September, and wild asters and golden-rod still bloomed on the roof. I was in what I thought of as Rebecca's garden, where the grass was being stubborn, trying to crowd out the small rose-bush Carl had planted and the oak sapling, sent by Olaf, that would someday shade the house. Inside, Inge was tending baby Jonathan. She was singing a Norwegian lullaby, and its melody set a meadowlark on our roof to singing. I tugged at a weed and then something, a shift of light, made me look up. There was a tiny figure against the vast background of the sky.

I sat back on my heels and arched my back, then glanced at the road—because now it was really a kind of road. More wagons passed day by day, headed to points west. Our place still boasted the only windmill in the county, but it was no longer the last frontier. Slowly the misty figure on the road resolved itself into the shape of a man. He was walk-ing with the morning sun behind him, and with the light in my eyes I couldn't make out his face at all.

He came into sharper focus, and I saw he was bearded and a little shabby. Since Jed Lynch, I'd grown a fear of strange men, but as he neared I noticed he walked an old man's gait. The tension in my shoulders eased. Still, I stood up, partly to see him better and partly to be able to run quickly into the house.

When the man saw me his pace quickened, and the sun slid behind a cloud. I watched, rooted to the spot. Something about his walk was familiar.

"Caitlin . . . Caitlin . . ."

At the sound of his voice, I thought I had truly gone mad. I put my hand to my cheeks. I pinched myself. I was indeed awake.

"Caitlin, is that you?"

"Pa? *Pa!*" And then my feet flew to him of their own accord, and moments later I was in my father's arms.

"You're alive!" I gasped. I pushed myelf back from him and took his face between my hands.

"I was rescued in the storm. But our ship was bound for China. It took months to get back, and the mail never reached you. When I got to New Bedford, all of you were gone—no one knew where, exactly. I went clear back to San Francisco and found Molly. She sent me to you."

I took his hands and kissed them. "I am so sorry, Pa. I am so sorry for everything that's happened."

"It's true Rebecca is gone, then."

I nodded.

"Molly told me." His eyes misted and he sighed, but then he looked at me with a sweet smile. "She told me I have a grandchild."

"Named after you," I was able to say now with

pride. "You will see him in a minute. But first you must meet Nate."

"Yes, she told me about that, too." He took my arm and squeezed it tight. "My little Caitlin is wed. Molly told me how I might love this place because it is like the sea. And she told me about the roof. Why, it really does grow flowers!"

That night we all stayed up talking until the moon set. Then Nate moved Jonathan's cradle out to the main room and set it up beside our bed. Pa bedded down in my old room. The first pale string of dawn, though far to the east, began to shine over the prairie, but I was too excited to sleep. Nate and I wandered out to the road and strode up the gentle slope of the cornfield. Brown stalks rustled beneath our feet as we walked.

At the top of the rise, we stopped, and faced east. As we watched, the sky brightened, first to pale gray, then pink, then a rich, warm peach. I was too full of joy for words. I felt I was in the middle of a miracle, and if I said too much I might break the spell. Nate moved behind me and circled me with his arms. He rested his chin on top of my head and buried his face in my hair.

"In my wildest dreams, Caitlin, I never imagined such happiness," he said, drawing me down beside him into the grass.

I closed my eyes a moment against the dawn. "Ssshh Nate," I silenced him. "I'm afraid it will all go away."

"It can't, Caitlin. Love like this is forever," he said just as the sun lifted over the horizon and the whole plain burst into birdsong.

I flung my arms around his neck and gazed up

into his blue-green eyes. They were so full of love, it took my breath away. Nate ran his hands through my hair, loosening my braid. Then he was kissing me all over. We held each other fiercely and kissed and touched until I thought I would melt into the very ground beneath us. When we finally parted to catch our breath, I pushed my hair out of my face.

"Look!" I cried. The roof of our house seem to burst into flame with the strong golden light of dawn. A solitary bird darted up from the sod roof like a small spark of light.

Nate and I watched as it vanished into the pale-blue sky. I suddenly thought of Rebecca, and knew Nate was right. Love truly was forever.

If you enjoyed *Plainsong for Caitlin*,

sample the following brief selection from

INTO THE WIND,

the next historical adventure in

American Dreams,

coming in May 1996 from Avon Flare.

Rosie looked toward the shore of Campeche, where, in the moonlight, she could make out the dim outlines of docked ships riding at anchor. She was exhausted and frightened and in pain, but still, she assessed the distance between herself and the side of the ship—calculating how fast she could cover the distance, how long it would take her to swim to shore. She winced involutarily at the thought of the saltwater on her burns, and thought it was probably just as well she didn't know how to swim.

"I wouldn't try it," Raider said softly. "I'd have you before you got anywhere near the rail."

She turned her back on him with all the dignity she could muster, adding a negligent little flounce for good measure, as if escape was the furthest thing from her mind.

As she watched, Baptiste emerged from the hatch. Behind him were two women. The first was as tall as Baptiste, slender and graceful in a seaman's trousers and striped shirt. Her face was a beautiful and serene oval, framed by long, loose waves of hair the color of the moonlight.

The other woman couldn't have been more different. She was shorter even than Rosie and twisted so that one shoulder was higher than the other. Her face was wizened like a dried apple, and a kerchief covered her hair. Her long blue skirt didn't disguise the fact that her feet were bare. Most remarkable of all, she was smoking a small clay pipe, and the friendly aroma of good Cuban tobacco spiced the air.

Rosie hastily shut her mouth, which she hadn't recalled opening. If she'd been ordered at gunpoint to choose a side to jump to, she wouldn't have been able to decide between the perils of the three strangers approaching her or those represented by Raider Lyons. It wasn't likely, though, that she would be offered any say in the matter.

"Raider," said the tall blond woman, her voice as low and smooth as water over stone. "I sent a boat to the *Avenger* as soon as we anchored, but you'd already gone ashore."

"Octavia," he said, coming to her and taking her in his arms, "I saw the *Ladyship* make anchor. I meant to come sooner, but circumstances intervened."

"How often they seem to do that with you," she said, pressing her cheek to his and closing her eyes. Raider held her and, as Rosie watched, every line of his long body relaxed. Why that should bother her, she couldn't begin to understand.

Raider drew back, still holding Octavia about the waist. Searching her face with his probing gaze, he asked, "Any news?"

She shook her head. "I saw LaFitte at The Cove six weeks ago. He says Governor Claiborne has declared him an outlaw and offered a five hundred dollar reward for his capture. But LaFitte has offered five *thousand* dollars for Governor Claiborne."

Raider laughed, an easy, almost boyish sound that couldn't have surprised Rosie more than if he had taken flight.

"He took two English supply ships," Octavia continued. "Prunes and tea and a hogshead of opium. Not much of that left by now, I'll wager, but plenty of prunes and tea."

Raider laughed again and, with one arm still around Octavia's waist, he bent and embraced the small gnarled woman. "Tuti," he said. "All is well with you?"

"To see you whole means all is well," she said.

Rosie watched, amazed. Where had this gentle, laughing boy come from? Where was the man who had killed her father and then calmly cracked a sailor across the face with the murder weapon? Or the man who had tried to frighten her with the pure force of his personality?

She sensed attention on her and turned to find Baptiste watching her. Slowly he winked one of his dark, liquid eyes and grinned his great white smile at her. Quickly, she looked down at her grimy toes.

As she studied the smooth deck between her feet, she felt Raider's hand on her arm. "This girl . . ."

he began and paused. "Let me see if I can remember all those names you have." He wrinkled his brow. "Rosalba—"

"Rosalia," she interrupted. "It's from my mother. She was Portuguese."

Everyone watched her in silence. Defiantly, she stared back.

"Forgive me," he said. "*Rosalia* Maria-Luisa Unity Fielding. Half English and, apparently, half Portuguese. Miss Fielding had the misfortune to be present at a tavern brawl that got out of hand. In the process, her father was killed and the tavern burned down. Unfortunately the tavern was also her home. She has some nasty burns on her legs, so I brought her here for Tuti to treat. Then you can decide what you want to do with her."

Octavia was studying Raider with eyes the blue-green color of the sea and every bit as intelligent as his. "What is there to decide?" she asked. "I've got no place for her on the *Ladyship*." She cast Rosie an acute, assessing glance and looked away again. Rosie felt as if she'd been measured and discarded. "What's your part in this, Raider?" Octavia asked.

"You sound like Nicodemus," Raider said, looking away from her. "I'm the one who killed her father." His set face showed no emotion. "Treat her burns and put her ashore."

Rosie's shoulders sagged with relief. She was not to be abandoned to a shipful of cutthroats after all.

"Why don't you take Tuti aboard the *Avenger?*" Octavia asked. "You need her more than I do. The *Ladyship* is too fast to get into many fights. You, on the other hand, go looking for them."

"Thank you, no," Raider said. "My men aren't

as enlightened as yours. They won't have a woman on board as part of the crew. Women as passengers or plunder are another matter, of course. If we have need of Tuti's help, we'll put in at The Cove and wait for you."

"You won't wait long. I stay close, usually. I'm only here because I was chased in by *Lightning*. I could have eluded her, but I knew I'd be safe in a neutral port and perhaps I would find word of you. It was a boon to find *Avenger* in the harbor."

Raider took hold of Octavia's shoulders and looked into her face. "God, I wish this would end." She nodded and he pressed his lips to her forehead and then to each cheek as Rosie watched, round-eyed. Octavia rested her head against Raider's shoulder for a moment, then straightened, raising her chin.

"When do you sail?" she asked.

"In an hour. I'd meant to leave this morning, but couldn't get the water loaded in time to catch the tide. Now I'm glad we waited."

"Be careful. Lawrence is always watching for you."

"And I him. Don't worry."

"You know how I hate to watch you sail," she said. "Godspeed." She turned and with quick steps crossed the deck, went down the hatch, and disappeared from sight.

Raider turned to Tuti, embraced her again, and said, "*Adieu*, Tuti."

He clapped Baptiste on the shoulder. "Stay ready."

Then he threw one long leg over the gunwale, looked at Rosie, and drew it back. He came to stand before her. "If our paths cross again, Nettle, I hope it's

161

under better circumstances. I regret your father's death.''

A remote kindness lurked in his eyes, in contrast to the resolute toughness of his young face; and his dark brows were drawn together in—in what? Concern? Puzzlement? Severity? She couldn't tell.

She lifted her face, smudged with soot and streaked with tears, and said with sincerity, ''Thank you.''

Gravely, he took a step closer to her. Then, taking her face into his hands, he leaned down and kissed her.

The warmth of his mouth on her cold lips was such a stunning surprise, such an explosive revelation, that Rosie had to grab handfuls of his linen shirtsleeves to keep herself from dropping straight to the deck of the *Ladyship*.

Even as she registered so many fresh and unique sensations, Raider ended the kiss. He paused for a moment, looking down into her face, and she could see the intelligence snapping like sparks in the depths of his hazel eyes. She was sure he could tell she had never before been kissed, as well as the effect his kiss had had on her, and she was mortified, for some unfathomable reason, by her lack of experience. She was further mortified at the thought that her breathing could probably be heard by the lookout at the top of the mainmast.

What she couldn't tell, from the composed arrangement of Raider's deliberately expressionless face, was the effect of the kiss on him.

As if to answer her, he lowered his mouth to hers again. This time he drew her closer to him, and she clutched even more desperately at the material of his shirt.

Abruptly he raised his head, breaking the kiss, and put her away from him.

She staggered a little, getting her balance, and then watched as he made a salute to those on the deck and flung himself over the gunwale, down the rope ladder, into the gig.

Look for All the Unforgettable Stories by Newbery Honor Author

★ AVI ★

THE TRUE CONFESSIONS OF CHARLOTTE DOYLE
71475-2/ $4.50 US/ $6.50 Can

NOTHING BUT THE TRUTH   71907-X/ $4.50 US/ $6.50 Can

THE MAN WHO WAS POE   71192-3/ $4.50 US/ $6.50 Can

SOMETHING UPSTAIRS   70853-1/ $4.50 US/ $6.50 Can

PUNCH WITH JUDY   72253-4/ $3.99 US/ $4.99 Can

A PLACE CALLED UGLY   72423-5/ $3.99 US/ $4.99 Can

SOMETIMES I THINK I HEAR MY NAME
72424-3/$3.99 US/ $4.99 Can

———————— And Don't Miss ————————

ROMEO AND JULIET TOGETHER (AND ALIVE!) AT LAST
70525-7/ $3.99 US/ $4.99 Can

S.O.R. LOSERS   69993-1/ $3.99 US / $4.99 Can

WINDCATCHER   71805-7/ $4.50 US/ $6.50 Can

BLUE HERON   72043-4 / $3.99 US/ $4.99 Can

"WHO WAS THAT MASKED MAN, ANYWAY?"
72113-9 / $3.99 US/ $4.99 Can

Avon Flare Presents
Powerful Novels
from Award-winning Authors

Joyce Carol Thomas

Bright Shadow	84509-1/$4.50 US/$6.50 Can
Marked by Fire	79327-X/$3.99 US/$4.99 Can

Alice Childress

A Hero Ain't Nothing But a Sandwich	
	00312-2/$4.50 US/$6.50 Can
Rainbow Jordan	58974-5/$3.99 US/$4.99 Can

Virginia Hamilton

Sweet Whispers, Brother Rush	
	65193-9/$4.50 US/$6.50 Can

Theodore Taylor

The Cay	01003-8/$4.50 US/$6.50 Can
Sniper	71193-1/$4.50 US/$6.50 Can
The Weirdo	72017-5/$4.50 US/$6.50 Can